A King Production presents...

DRAKE

A NOVEL

JOY DEJA KING
AND CHRIS BOOKER

ISBN 13: 978-0991389018
ISBN 10: 0991389018
Cover concept by Joy Deja King
Cover Model: Joy Deja King

Library of Congress Cataloging-in-Publication Data;
A King Production
Drake by: Joy Deja King and Chris Booker
For complete Library of Congress Copyright info visit;
www.joydejaking.com

A King Production
P.O. Box 912, Collierville, TN 38027
A King Production and the above portrayal log are trademarks of
A King Production LLC

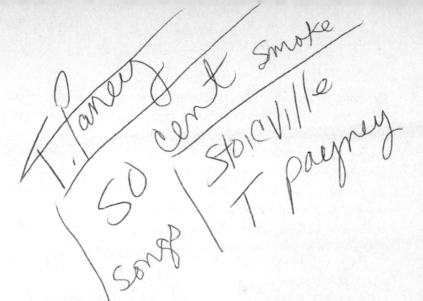

This Book is Dedicated To My:

Family, Readers and Supporters.
I LOVE you guys so much. Please believe that!!

"Who shot me, but you punks didn't finish/Now you're 'bout to feel the wrath of a Menace."

— Tupac

Prologue

"Push! Push!" the doctor directed Kim, as he held the top of the baby's head, hoping this would be the final push that would bring a new life into the world.

The hospital's delivery room was packed with both Kim and Drake's family, and although the large crowd irritated Drake, he still managed to video record the birth of his son. After four hours of labor, Kim gave birth to a 6.5-pound baby boy, whom they already named Derrick Jamal Henson Jr. Drake couldn't help but to shed a few tears of joy at the new addition to his family, but the harsh reality of his son's safety quickly replaced his joy with anger.

Drake was nobody's angel and beyond his light brown eyes and charming smile, he was one of the most feared men in the city of Philadelphia, due to his street credentials. He put a lot of work in on the blocks of South Philly, where he grew up. He mainly pushed drugs and gambled, but from time to time he'd place well-known dealers into the trunk of his car and hold them for ransom, according to how much that person was worth.

"I need everybody to leave the room for awhile," Drake told the people in the hospital room, wanting to share a private moment alone with Kim and his son.

The families took a few minutes saying their good-byes, before leaving. Kim and Drake sat alone in the room, rejoicing over the birth of baby Derrick. The only interruption was doctors coming in and out of the room, to check up on the baby, mainly because they were a little concerned about his breathing. The doctor informed Drake that he would run a few more tests to make sure the baby would be fine.

"So, what are you going to do?" Kim questioned Drake, while he was cradling the baby.

"Do about what?" he shot back, without lifting his head up. Drake knew what Kim was alluding to, but he had no interest in discussing it. Once Kim became pregnant, Drake agreed to leave the street life alone, if not completely then significantly cutting back, after their baby was born. They both feared if he didn't stop living that street life, he would land in the box. Drake felt he and jail were like night and day: they could never be together.

"You know what I'm talking about, Drake. Don't play stupid with me," Kim said, poking him in his head with her forefinger.

He smiled. "I gave you my word I was out of the game when you had our baby. Unless my eyes are deceiving me, I think what I'm holding in my arms is our son. Just give me a couple days to clean up the streets and then we can sit down and come up with a plan on how to invest the money we got."

Cleaning up the streets meant selling all the drugs he had and collecting the paper owed to him from his workers and guys he fronted weight to. All together there was about 100k due, not to mention the fact he had to appoint someone to take over his bread-winning crack houses and street corners that made him millions of dollars.

Drake's thoughts came to a halt when his phone started to ring. Sending the call straight to voicemail didn't help any, because it rang again. Right when he reached to turn the phone off, he noticed it was Peaches calling. If it were anybody else, he probably would've declined, but Peaches wasn't just anybody.

"Yo," he answered, shifting the baby to his other arm, while trying to avoid Kim's eyes cutting over at him.

"He knows! He knows everything!" Peaches yelled, with terror in her voice.

Peaches wasn't getting good reception out in the woods, where Villain had left her for dead, so the words Drake was hearing were broken up. All he understood was "Villain knows!" That was enough to get his heart racing. His heart wasn't racing out of fear, but rather excitement.

In many ways, Villain and Drake were cut from the same cloth. They even both shared tattoos of several teardrops under their eyes. It seemed like gunplay was the only thing that turned Drake on—besides fucking—and when he could feel it in the air, murder was the only thing on his mind.

Drake hung up the phone and tried to call Peaches back to see if he could get better reception, but her phone went straight to voicemail. Damn! He thought to himself as he tried to call her back repeatedly and block out Kim's voice as she steadily asked him if everything was all right.

"Drake, what's wrong?"

"Nothing, I gotta go. I'll be back in a couple of hours," he said, handing Kim their son.

"How sweet! There's nothing like family!" said a voice coming from the direction of the door.

Not yet lifting his head up from his son to see who had entered the room, at first Drake thought it was a doctor, but once the sound of the familiar voice kicked in, Drake's heart began beating at an even more rapid pace. He turned to see Villain standing in the doorway, chewing on a straw and clutching what appeared to be a gun at his waist. Drake's first instinct was to reach for his own weapon, but remembering that he left it in the car made his insides burn. Surely, if he had his gun on him, there would have been a showdown right there in the hospital.

"Can I come in?" Villain asked, in an arrogant tone, as he made his way over to the visitors' chairs. "Let me start off by saying congratulations on having a bastard child."

Villain's remarks made Drake's jaw flutter continuously from fury. Sensing shit was about to go left, Kim attempted to get out of the bed with her baby to leave the room, but before her feet could hit the floor, Villain pulled out a .50 Caliber Desert Eagle and placed it on his lap. The gun was so enormous that Drake could damn near read off the serial number on the slide. Kim looked at the nurse's button and was tempted to press it.

"Push the button and I'll kill all three of y'all. Scream and I'ma kill all three of y'all. Bitch," Villian paused, making sure the words sunk in, "if you even blink the wrong way, I'ma kill all three of y'all."

"What the fuck you want?" Drake asked, still trying to be firm in his speech.

"You know, at first, I thought about getting my money back and then killin' you, for setting my brother up wit' those bitches you got working for you. But on my way here I just said, 'Fuck the money!' I just wanna kill the nigga."

Deep down inside, Drake wanted to ask for his life to be spared, but his pride wouldn't allow it. Not even the fact that his newborn son was in the room could make Drake beg to stay alive, which made Villain even more eager to lullaby his ass into a permanent sleep.

Villain wanted to see the fear in his eyes before he pulled the trigger, but Drake was a G, and was bound to play that role 'til he kissed death.

Chapter 1

TWO MONTHS EARLIER

The sounds of gunshots filled the air as the day was winding down at the Last Shot Gun Range, which for some reason seemed crowded for a Sunday. Sunday was the day Drake and Peaches took off to tighten up on their shooting. Plus, there was something about firing a gun that relieved stress for the both of them after a long week. It was at this very range nine months ago that Drake and Peaches met for the first time. The mutual feeling they shared for guns is what brought them together, and the ambition to take over the world is what made them closer.

In booth five, Peaches stood there wearing a pair of skintight, light-blue jeans, a white tank top, and a pair of designer six-inch heels that seemed much better suited for a nightclub. Over her eyes was a pair of Bvlgari shield pink gold with gloss black sunglasses. Her jet-black curls framed her flawless deep chocolate skin, and she was clutching a .45 ACP, firing at her target.

"Did you take care of what I asked you to?" Drake asked, sliding up behind her while she fired at the target.

"Yeah. I called Ralph, and he said everything was a go for next Thursday. I told him that you would call him Tuesday."

"What about you? Are you ready for this?" Drake asked, lowering her weapon and turning her to face him.

This was a big sting for a lot of money, and Drake couldn't afford to mess this up. It could cost them their lives if something was to go wrong.

Peaches had set plenty of niggas up for the take-down, and she was good at what she did, but Tazz wasn't the one you get caught slippin' with. Tazz was the type to kill you in front of a hundred people, drag your body to the middle of the street, stand on top of it like he was King Kong, and dare anyone to say anything. It was rumored that he killed his father when he was eight years old because his dad used to beat up on his mom. He never shed a tear on the day of the funeral. People really thought he was possessed by the devil.

The one thing about Tazz was that he had money stacked to the ceiling. His dope was so pure that people thought he manufactured it himself. If everything worked out as planned, the take on this robbery would be in the millions.

"You know we still got some homework to do," Drake continued. "I want you to go buy a couple of burn-out cell phones, and go buy something super sexy for the bedroom." He wrapped his arms around her waist and pressed his dick up against her ass.

Although Drake had a main chick named Kim, Peaches had grabbed a piece of his heart over time, but they had an understanding. Peaches could fuck whomever she wanted as long as Drake and Kim stayed together. He had three simple rules for Peaches, and as long as these rules didn't get violated he would never turn his back on her:

Rule number one was that besides her, Drake came first. Rule number two was that Drake was the only one who went inside of her raw; i.e. without a condom, and that included that his dick was the only one she sucked. The third rule was that Peaches couldn't ever lie to him.

He figured that if she would lie then she'd cheat, and if she cheated, she'd steal. None of the three were acceptable, and none of it really mattered, because all Peaches wanted to do was be with Drake. She realized he was with her most of the time, so she felt confident that she was actually number one. Peaches couldn't even bring herself to give up the pussy to anybody other than Drake anyway.

"What about Ralph?" Peaches asked in a concerned manner. "I really don't trust dat muthafucker. He knows I'm ya girl, but he keeps running dat old ass bullshit game on me like I'm suppose to bite."

"Ralph ain't nothin', but a puppet. After the score, I'll take care of him. Just play it cool in the meantime, and show da nigga a titty every now and again to keep him happy," Drake whispered in her ear jokingly, making her laugh thinking that's all it took to get Ralph excited.

A police car had been sitting on the corner of 23rd Street near Tasker Avenue for the past two days, slowing up a lot of money for Cindy. This street was her gold mine because every crack-head from 32nd Street to 16th Street came and copped there, including a few out-of-towners who preferred to buy a little weight. Twenty-third Street alone pulled in about fifteen thousand a shift, with three shifts a day. It was hard for smokers to resist the best coke in the city, and with that, a lot of jealousy was raised from the dead.

Cindy literally took over South Philly in the early 2000s, and had no plans on loosening up her grip when she inherited the drug business from her father, Mark, after he was killed in front of her during a home invasion. Niggas in the hood respected her G when she rocked to sleep the same dudes who shot Mark, leaving a small trail of unsolved homicides in her path. People in the hood had love for Mark, and when they finally got a chance to meet Cindy, they could see a lot of Mark in her. The old saying, "A woman is a reflection of her man," which in this case meant Cindy's father was true, and everybody felt the same way, even Chris, a relentless rival. Cindy inherited more than just the drug business from her father. She also inherited his beef/competition.

Cindy pulled up to 23rd Street in a silver, tricked out Range Rover. She couldn't help but, notice the cop car sitting on the corner, so she called Lil' Rick, one of the three workers she had on this shift. Before she could dial the number, Rick came out of a house on the block.

Cindy was no stranger to the streets, so when she stepped out of the truck, a couple of kids that were playing on the sidewalk spoke to her as she walked towards Rick. The sun glistened off of her caramel complexion, as she walked on the sidewalk with her Jeffrey Campbell's Popp sneakers. The kick-ass shoes featured gold hardware lace, black velcro buckles, gold lettering, and hot pink lining with a zip closure on the side. She paired the look with some cutoff jean shorts, a tank top and her hair was slicked back in a ballerina bun. Although she was casually dressed, her diamond studs, expensive purse that hung on her shoulder, and iced out wrist let you know Cindy's coins were very long.

"The block is hot right now," Rick said, meeting her at the mom and pop store on the corner. "The nigga, Chris, been sending shooters through here every day for three days straight, trying to rob the workers. My man, P., that works the night shift shot one of them last night."

"What about the cops?" Cindy inquired, seeing the lack of money being made.

"At first they just passed through when they got a report of gunshots being fired, but ever since last night one cop car just sits on the corner all day. The guy that P. shot almost bled to death and it drew a big crowd. The shit was all over the news and everything."

Even though the cops were sitting on the corner, crack-heads were still bold enough to come down the street, so the workers were bold enough to make a few sales behind parked cars. Money was being made, but it had slowed down considerably.

Cindy was feeling some type of way that business wasn't booming. Although 23rd Street was her main strip, it wasn't her only one. Because it was an established spot, she was optimistic things would pick back up soon. But now that Chris came out of his shell, it was about time that Cindy made the streets remember who she was and the consequences that came with crossing her.

"Look, I want everybody to fall back for a couple of days so the heat can cool down. I don't want anybody selling a single rock out here. We'll open up shop in a couple of days," she explained to Rick. "We got to get these guys off the corner," she said, nodding in the direction of the cop car.

Cindy jumped back into her truck, and before she pulled off, she called D-Rock, an old-timer who rolled with her dad when he was alive. D-Rock was a legend in the hood, and everybody respected him mainly because he still put in work at the age of fifty. He wasn't a hit man for Cindy, but rather an advisor and a friend that she could talk to about almost anything. After her dad died, D-Rock basically raised her from the age of 17. Despite the fact that Cindy was one of the biggest drug dealers in the city, D-Rock had love for her and became a father figure in her life.

DRAKE

The small crew Tazz kept around him was about their business when it came to gunplay, Drake thought to himself after noticing two out of five men that surrounded Tazz in front of the club he owned.

Drake had been following Tazz around for the past two days, trying to see any patterns in his movements that could be useful. There wasn't anything unusual or useful, and even though Drake already knew where Tazz lived, he hadn't been home in two days.

Villain was the first person Drake noticed. He was sitting on the hood of a BMW 7 Series Sedan with Tazz. He knew Villain from a couple years back. They were fuckin' the same chick at one point, and she used to tell Drake all about how crazy Villain was and who the latest victim was that he shot. It seemed like every time Drake went to fuck the broad, she had a new story about the dude.

Drake's phone began to vibrate with an incoming call. It was Kim. He thought about answering it, but he was stalking his prey at the moment and wanted no interruptions. He had to stay focused. If Drake made the wrong move and Tazz had any idea that he was two blocks away watching him, Tazz would have somebody come light the car up with bullets before he got a chance to pull off. Besides, Drake was about to head home in a couple of hours because being outside for two days without a shower and a good night's sleep could take a toll on anybody.

The second person he noticed in the crew was Ice. Drake knew Ice from the county jail about a year back. Ice was fighting a double homicide while Drake was fighting an attempted murder charge. Everyone knew that Ice killed the people he was locked up for, but no-body was willing to take the chance on testifying against him. Drake beat his case before Ice did, so when he got released from county that was the last time he saw him until now. From the looks of things, Ice beat his case, too.

Drake's phone started vibrating again. This time it was Ralph, and this wasn't a call he could ignore. Looking around his car at empty potato chip bags and empty soda cans, he found his phone under the trash. "Yo, holla at ya boy."

"What's good, Drake? Can you meet me right now?"

"Give me the place," Drake said, starting his car with intentions on leaving.

"The McDonald's on Broad Street, in two hours," Ralph said, then hung up the phone.

Just when Drake was about to pull off, he saw a dark-colored Benz pull up in front of the club, and out jumped a woman with a bag in her hand. Instead of pulling off, Drake grabbed the binoculars to get a better look at what was going on. The bag looked like it had some weight to it. Tazz quickly grabbed the bag from her and took it into the club.

Drake pulled off, wondering what could be in the bag. He didn't know if it was money, drugs, or just nothing at all, but for now it was time to get home, take a shower, and then go meet up with Ralph. Sleep was not an option today; and if money were on the line, Drake would always push it to the limit.

Chapter 2

Cindy walked into the lounge which wasn't that crowded—at least at the bar—but she knew where everybody was; most importantly, where Chris was. She sat at the bar and ordered a double shot of Christian Brothers while taking a good look around for an emergency exit if needed. The bartender, Ms. Patty, knew Cindy from the neighborhood, but none of that really mattered because Cindy was on a mission.

She threw back her double shot then headed for the ladies' room. Before pulling out a .357 Magnum from her waistband, she checked the stalls to make sure no one else was in the bathroom, but her. She then placed the gun on the sink while she put her hair into a ponytail. The all black getup made it clear what Cindy's intentions were, at least in her mind it did… it meant murder.

"Seven! Seven, my nigga!" Chris yelled out as the dice hit up against the wall. While he snatched the money off the floor, the sound of the bathroom door opening and closing caught the attention of everybody in the room. It got so quiet that you could hear the light noise coming from the air-conditioner blowing through the vent.

Cindy kept her back against the bathroom door, keeping everybody in sight directly in front of her. She looked down at Chris who was getting up from the floor with a smile on his face after seeing that it was Cindy.

"Draw, nigga!" Cindy said, pulling her pistol from her waistband and holding it against her thigh.

It could have been easy for her to shoot Chris before he had a chance to pull out his gun, but the rush she got from squaring off like an old western flick was more desirable. She wanted to make a point that besides her being a woman, she could bang with the best of men. Respect is what she wanted, and respect was what she was going to get. Cindy needed to set an example and Chris was her mark.

At first, Chris didn't take her seriously. In fact, he reached for the dice and thought about rolling them. But once he zoomed in to Cindy's face, he recognized that all too familiar gaze of murder in her eyes. He rocked that exact gaze right before he was about to take a life, too. Chris glanced over at two of his boys, and without a word being said they pulled guns out from their waistbands and pointed them at Cindy.

"Come on, shorty. You really wanna go through with this?" Chris asked, now pulling a .9mm from his waist. "How about you put yo' gun away, we go out to the bar, have a couple drinks, and we can talk about what got you so mad," he said sarcastically.

The talking is over, Cindy thought to herself. She was tired of losing money and them going back and forth shooting up one another's blocks making South Philly hot. This side of the city wasn't big enough for the both of them, so Cindy made her ultimatum: Do or die.

"Fuck it!" she said, smacking the light switch off and leaving the room pitch black.

Silence took over the room once again for a split second until the sound of the .357 hammer cocking back broke it. Then all hell broke loose.

Cindy fired the first shot, lighting up the room from the blast. The flash gave her enough light to see Chris's position, but before she could get another shot off, his boys started shooting wildly in her direction. With shots being fired, nobody could see anything nor reach for the door. The only thing that could happen was for everybody to fire at one another until no one had any bullets left, and that's exactly what happened.

Cindy got low to the ground and let off the remainder of her shots in the direction of where the other gun flashes were coming from. A bullet hit Chris in the neck and he screamed from the heat it brought with it.

The shots stopped and silence took over the room once again. Cindy could feel a burning sensation in her stomach and figured that one of the bullets went through her vest. She got up and reached for the door, found the knob and opened it to let some light into the room. Before limping out, she could see Chris lying on the floor and holding his neck. The two guys who pulled out guns first were also lying on the floor holding their chests and arms. Everybody else lay on the floor shocked, but still alive.

Cindy stumbled to the front door while holding her stomach. She fell to her knees, but got back up to her feet and made it out to the sidewalk. Traffic was moving pretty fast on Broad Street where the bar was located, and it would take a miracle to get across the street to her car, or at least a red light to stop the cars.

Seeing one of the guys come out motivated Cindy to take her chances on dodging traffic to get to her vehicle. While darting across the street, a hail of bullets followed her, knocking holes in parked cars and shattering windows along the way. Rob, who was only shot in the arm, managed to find a gun with some bullets in it and wasted no time trying to kill Cindy.

Bringing cars to a screeching halt from falling to the ground, Cindy started going in and out of consciousness and losing a lot of blood in the process. With an empty .357 clutched in her hand, she lay on the ground, unable to run any further. She could hear cars slowing down and blowing their horns, and then she could see Rob making his way across the street.

Suddenly the miracle she needed pulled up right beside her face, coming between her and absolute death. She took one last look at her stomach, then passed out. It was over. Only God could save her now.

Chapter 3

Veronica walked into the bank, equipped with a smile and an ink pen, ready to make her withdrawal for the day. The security guards watched as she strutted across the lobby floor with the sort of body video vixens strived for.

"Good morning, my name is Christina Fields. I believe I spoke to you over the phone yesterday about making a withdrawal today," Veronica spoke softly to the bank manager.

The manager knew exactly who she was, remembering that she wanted to withdraw thirty thousand dollars from her joint bank account with her husband. She wanted to verify they would have the money on hand because most people didn't withdraw that much cash in a single transaction.

"Yes, good morning Mrs. Fields, I'm glad you could come in today. Can I have your identification?" the manager asked while escorting her to his office.

Veronica provided the manager with the fake driver's license Drake gave her, including a birth certificate, and Social Security card. Everything checked out, and although identity theft was at an alarmingly high rate at the banks, the manager never suspected anything. He asked a few questions—which was routine—and after she answered them with ease, everything else was simple.

"How would you like the bills?"

"It doesn't matter. It'll all spend the same way," she replied with a smile on her face.

Drake sat outside in the car waiting for Veronica. He knew that she was good at what she did, but just in case, he left the car running.

He and Veronica went all the way back to childhood. Drake growing up with a single mother and Veronica with a single father, their parents dated each other a few times, but never became anything more than just friends, and that's exactly the relationship Drake and Veronica had.

Back when Veronica was a teenager she used to boost high-priced clothes from big department stores, then turn around and sell them to her girlfriends for a cheaper price. It was only when she met Patricia Goldstein, a computer geek in her first year of college that she began to use other women's personal information to apply for credit cards and open up fraudulent bank accounts. Once she became familiar with the unlimited bounties of the World Wide Web, there wasn't a woman in America that Veronica couldn't depict.

Veronica walked out of the bank toting a Louis Vuitton carry bag on her shoulder with a cool thirty grand in it. She even managed to transfer an additional twenty grand into a separate account from Christina Fields' husband. She also got a printout of Tazz's account balance and a few credit card numbers that Tazz's wife, Christina, used on a daily basis. Veronica's motto was: "You go hard or go broke."

Drake had called Veronica about a week ago telling her how he had some work for her, and the numbers involved were six figures or better. There wasn't much more to say, mainly because it was coming from Drake, and if Drake had a scheme, it was going to be worth it. Anything he fucked with turned out to be lucrative, and being that he was a good friend, Veronica knew he wouldn't have her on a crash dummy mission.

"You're not gonna believe this shit," Veronica said, getting into the car. "This nigga got money." She passed Drake the printout. "Plus, I transferred another twenty thousand into another account," she went on, while Drake looked at the paper.

"Damn! Four point seven million!" he mumbled to himself, surprised it was more than what he thought it would be.

"He also has another account separate from this one. I think it's a business account, but I can't get access to it; or should I say his wife can't get access to it. He only gives her access to this account." Veronica pointed out, plucking the piece of paper in Drake's hand.

"So, how much do you think you can drain before he finds out what's going on?"

"Well, his wife has joint access to this account, which means they don't have to contact him every time she makes a withdrawal. The only problem is that anything over fifty thousand dollars, both parties have to be contacted and agree upon the transaction. That's why I only took thirty thousand in cash, and transferred the other twenty thousand to another account."

"So, how much can you take?" Drake asked again, amused by all the banking talk.

"Given the fifty thousand dollar credit limit on the credit card, and the fifty thousand a day cash limit, I know I could get 100k a day from him as long as he and his wife stay busy enough not to pay attention to the account."

"Well, how do you plan on using up the credit card limit without a credit card?"

Veronica reached into her bag and pulled out a brand new MasterCard that she had gotten while she was in the bank. She gave the manager a sad story about how she was drunk one night and cut up her credit card. Money hungry banks never have a problem helping you fuck up your credit, so a new credit card was happily issued. She also pulled out the thirty grand and gave it to Drake, since the plan was to split the profit 60/40.

"What's this?" Drake asked, taking the money without even counting it.

"That's 30k. I put my cut into another account, remember? I can go get that anytime. The account I sent it to, the bank will never be able track it. I'll pick it up later on. For now, we got some shopping to do," Veronica said with a smile on her face, holding up the credit card.

"Yeah, look, I'ma drop you off to your car because I got to take care of a few things, so I can't go wit' you. Just make sure you buy small shit like jewelry; something we can get rid of without a problem. Call me later on and let me know what time you want me to pick you up in the morning. We got a lot of work to do in a little bit of time."

Drake dropped Veronica off and headed home, hoping that Kim wouldn't be mad that he had missed her starring in a play last night. He didn't even call to let her know he wasn't going to make it. Following Tazz around all night caused him to forget that shit.

Kim was Drake's heart. They had been together for a couple of years now and had been living with one another for the past six months after Kim found out she was pregnant. She was a paralegal, working in the biggest law firm in Philadelphia, so Drake was always up on the new laws that were passed by Congress.

Although she was with child, at night Kim attended Performing Arts School. She was somewhat far along in her pregnancy, but was barely showing and had recently landed a role in a stage play that had a two-day run. It was 2:00 p.m., and the last showing was at 6:00 p.m. Drake had to rush home and take a quick shower, so he would be able to escort Kim. His night was pretty much cut out, and by no means would Kim let him go back outside after they made it home from the play.

Golden climbed to the top of the pole, turned upside down and slid with her legs in a split while making her butt cheeks clap until she reached the bottom.

It was audition day at the Coffee Cup Gentlemen's Club for exotic dancers, and Tazz, along with Villain, were the only judges for today. They were sitting in the front row and enjoying watching the 20 new dancers work the pole giving their best stripper moves.

"We got a shipment coming in on Friday," Tazz commented to Villain, not taking his eyes off of Apple, who was dancing on the stage with Golden.

Villain was Tazz's right hand man, and Tazz put him in charge of the drug trafficking aspect of the business. It was one less thing that Tazz had to worry about during his day-to-day operations. With all three gentlemen's clubs, two restaurants, and two daycare centers, he needed some help maintaining the streets. Trust was big with Tazz, and there weren't many people he trusted. He knew Villain since the second grade, and up until now, at the age of thirty, they have been rolling tight.

"Yeah, ya boy, Blue Black, been calling me all day. He needed like twenty-five birds to fly his way. New York ain't got shit right now," Villain said, writing down the names of the strippers he liked for the club. "I got thirty bricks left from the last shipment so I can serve him if you want me to. I didn't know if you wanted me to hold onto it until we get right again like the last time."

"Nah, that's cool. But tell Blue that I need 18.5 this time around. Da price of this shit is going up for me, so it's definitely going up for him. Tell him to get his money up. The more he cops, the cheaper it gets."

Tazz had a connection in Cuba who could get the coke into the United States for a low price, just as long as the trip was worth it. He was buying 200 bricks a month for 2.1 million of pure cocaine. Now the price went up to 2.5 million for 200 bricks, plus an additional 100k to get it safely delivered to the city. That personal door service made that extra price well worth it.

"I swear, Villain, it won't be much longer until I fall back completely from this drug game. It ain't that I'm tired of the streets, it's just that I feel like I'm ready to step my game up and touch some of this corporate money."

"You tryin' to go legal on me, Tazz?" Villain asked jokingly, throwing a couple fifty-dollar bills on the stage at Peppermint, another new dancer.

"Who the hell told you corporate money was legal money?" Tazz shot back. They both busted out laughing.

Tazz could never leave the streets alone completely, no matter how many times he said he would. After all, it was the streets that got him to where he was at right now. More or less, he really just wanted to broaden his horizons and see if his money was long enough to gain some respect in the corporate world. The clubs, restaurants, and daycare centers were just a front to hide his drug affiliation ties with the Cubans. He mainly let his wife run all the businesses while he and Villain fucked the city with no condoms; with the best cocaine to hit this side of America.

All conversation came to a complete halt when Peaches took the stage, wearing a naughty nurse lingerie one piece and a pair of high heels. Her thighs were thick, fat ass, stomach flat, and her face was pretty. She was mesmerizing everybody who looked at her; even the last dancer, Peppermint, stopped to watch her moves on the pole. Tazz and Villain were so caught up in her beauty that they didn't even notice she wasn't really dancing. Rather, she was just swaying her hips from side to side in a sexy motion.

"Who the hell is that?" Tazz asked Villain, picking his mouth up off the floor.

"Stand down, big fella. Christine will kill you," Villain joked.

"Nigga, there ain't a bitch that danced on my stage I didn't fuck. Those are the perks of being the boss," Tazz joked back before getting up from his seat and walking up to the stage to talk to Peaches.

"Play on, playa! Play on!" Villain laughed while watching his sidekick.

Villain's phone began to ring. It was Blue texting him in code. He was still trying to score, and now that Villain had the okay to serve him, money was always over bitches. He got up from the table, smiling at Tazz whispering sweet nothings in Peaches ear.

Before going home, Drake stopped by the hospital, hoping that the mystery girl had awakened from her coma. A couple nights ago when he was on his way to meet Ralph at the Broad Street McDonald's, he saw a woman darting across the street, almost getting hit by a couple of cars in the process. Seeing the girl was holding her stomach and clutching a large revolver, Drake pulled up next to her, mostly because the traffic light was turning red. Focused on her, he didn't even notice the guy coming across the street with a gun pointed in his direction. He got out of the car with a gun in his hand just in case he had to use it. He turned around when he heard someone walking up behind him and saw Rob was squeezing the trigger of his gun.

It could have only been the will of God that Rob ran out of bullets before he made it across the street to where Cindy and Drake were.

Out of instinct, Drake fired a couple shots at Rob, one that hit his leg, making Rob turn around and run. Thinking fast, Drake scooped Cindy up and put her in the back seat of his car. She kept going in and out of shock and saying, "No hospitals!"

Drake had been in this situation before, so he knew that if he took her to a nearby hospital, she would probably end up in jail after she was treated. He ripped off his T-shirt and tied it around her waist where she was shot so it would slow the bleeding down enough for him to get her to a hospital outside of the city. Unfortunately, New Jersey was the closest hospital outside of the city, and being that the expressway was two blocks away, it wouldn't take but 20 minutes to get there. He didn't know if she would make it through the ride, but he took the chance anyway.

Drake walked into the hospital room, and to his surprise Cindy was awake and sitting up in bed. He could see that she was in some pain, but she was alive. When she turned and saw Drake entering the room, Cindy had a look of fear on her face, as if he was there to finish the job.

At that moment, D-Rock walked out of the room's bathroom and noticed the look on Cindy's face. D-Rock quickly put his hand on his waist, reaching for his gun. "What do you want?" he questioned Drake, ready and willing to draw his weapon.

"Well, I just stopped by to see how Cindy was doing. She bled all over my back seats a couple nights ago. I thought I would at least come by to see if she was still alive," Drake said, slowly reaching in his pocket and pulling out Cindy's ID and handing it to her.

Cindy looked closely at Drake, but she couldn't remember his face from that night. The fact that she kept going in and out of consciousness prevented her from remembering much of anything that happened that night. She couldn't remember how she had gotten to the hospital or who brought her here. All she knew was that someone from that lounge had shot her. "So, it was you who brought me here?" she asked, grabbing her ID from Drake.

"Yeah, and I got a heavy car detailing bill to prove it. You know, you lost a lot of blood. How are you?" he asked, genuinely concerned.

Cindy apologized for her rudeness and introduced Drake to D-Rock, but Drake already knew who D-Rock was from the neighborhood. That's the reason why he didn't make any false moves when D-Rock came out of the bathroom. Even though he didn't know him personally, growing up in South Philly he heard the stories about D-Rock.

"Let me ask you something. Why did you help me? You don't even know me," she said, very curious about his actions.

Even Drake didn't know why he had helped her. He had no business to pull over and get in between her and a gun. But for some reason he felt sad for her, lying on the ground while cars just zoomed past without stopping to help her. It just seemed like the right thing to do at the time. "I don't know why I helped you. I never did no shit like that before. I'm from the hood, and hood niggas don't chew on other nigga's beef. The good thing is that you're still alive. That's the only reason why I came here. I wanted to make sure you didn't die."

Drake couldn't stick around for too much longer. He didn't want to be late getting home. He found out a few things about Cindy from the guys in the neighborhood and was shocked that she had a part of South Philly on lock down. Drake was from the same part of Philly, but most of his business was done in West or North Philly, so he was kind of out of touch with everything that went down in her part of the hood; but after saving Cindy's life and finding out they both were heavy in the streets, he felt this wasn't the last time their paths would cross.

Peaches was in the dressing room changing back into her clothes when Tazz walked in with the list of names of who had gotten the job. He called out seven names, including hers, and gave them the option to start work tonight. Not at all shocked that she was picked, Peaches pulled Tazz to the side for a solo conversation. Wanting to hear what she had to say, he excused himself from the other women.

"I appreciate you picking me for the job, but I'm really not too interested in being a dancer. I only came here to support my girlfriend, Rose, and to have a little fun at the same time."

Tazz cut Peaches off before she could say anything else. He paused to think for a second before he spoke, stepping back and taking a good look at how beautiful she was. From the moment she stepped on the stage, he was open. His wife looked good, but Peaches was pure beauty at its best. And if there were any kind of woman he would have an ongoing affair on his wife with, it would be Peaches. He figured that he had to do something to keep her around. "I don't want you to be a dancer," he said with a smile on his face, "I want you to be my hostess."

"Your hostess?" Peaches questioned with confusion on her face.

"Yeah. We get some high profile people coming through my doors, and I think a pretty face like yours greeting them could really class the place up. Plus, I'll make sure to make it worth your while financially."

Peaches had Tazz right where she wanted him. She really didn't want to be a dancer, but having access to the club was needed, and keeping a close eye on Tazz was a plus as well. By the lust in his eyes, Peaches knew for sure that she could get more out of him than he could get out of her.

The only tricky part about being around him was that he was fine, sexy, and had money. She couldn't help but to notice his strong build, thick full lips, dark chocolate skin, and the bulge in his pants that stood out... literally!

"I'll take the job, if you could get me an escort to and from the club. I take the bus to school, but I refuse to ride one at night. I can't be traveling solo after dark. There are too many crazy people out here," Peaches said in a sweet yet sassy voice.

"No problem. I'll have Ice escort you around until we can get you a car."

"I can't drive. I don't know how to."

"No problem. I'll make Ice your personal driver. I got a party tomorrow night. Some rappers and ball players will be in the building. Can you make it?"

Peaches thought about it for a moment. Friday is the day that she and Drake were going to Atlantic City for the weekend. She didn't want to spend her night hosting some thirsty rappers and asshole athletes who think that every chick in the club want them so they should be able to grab on your ass for free. Them tips might not be worth my time. On the other hand, Drake might want me to see if I could find out more info on Tazz, she reasoned. "Yeah, I can work tomorrow. What time will Ice come pick me up?" she asked, writing down a bogus address and giving it to Tazz.

"He'll pick you up around 9:00 p.m. Dress sexy, but don't show too much, just enough to give people something to look at. I'll see you tomorrow."

Veronica wasted no time in finding her way to Tiffany's jewelry store. As soon as she walked through the door, she spotted a ring behind the glass with a rock the size of a skittle in it. The price tag on the ring was 10k, and without thinking twice she told the sales clerk that she wanted to purchase it, along with the diamond bracelet next to it that cost 20k. It was like being a kid in a candy store except with somebody else's money.

She thought about what Drake said, buying something small on the credit card that they could get rid of easily, but that was only for his cut, not hers.

It was getting kind of late to be going to the mall or for cruising South Street, a strip where there's nothing but clothing stores. For tonight, Tiffany's had to do, and as badly as she wanted a 60-inch flat screen TV with a surround sound system, she had to stick to the plan Drake had for right now. She bought another diamond ring, diamond earrings and a pink diamond necklace to match. The total came up to 48 thousand.

Veronica found it easy being Christine Fields, spending 48k in one store in less than twenty minutes. She even left a couple thousand on the credit card just in case the real Christine needed to purchase something that day.

The money was good and fast, just the way she liked it, but she knew there had to be a way she could get more out of the bank account than 100k a day. The first person that came to mind that could help her, if there was any way it could be done, was her old friend, Patricia Goldstein.

Leaving Tiffany's, Veronica looked through her phone to see if Patricia's number was still in it, and she prayed that she hadn't changed her number. It had been a while since Veronica spoke to her, but she knew that if she needed her, she would be there in the drop of a dime, especially when money was involved.

Good. Her number is still in here, Veronica thought to herself, pressing the call button in hopes that Pat would answer.

"Hell must have frozen over!" Patricia said, answering her phone, and shocked that her caller ID indicated that Veronica was calling.

"Not hell but a free flowing river of money and of course I wanted to share the wealth." Veronica beamed.

Chapter 4

Drake walked through the door only to be yelled at by Kim, who was sitting in the living room getting her hair done by her girlfriend, Monica. It was a little after 4:00 and he still had to take a shower, get dressed and be out the door by 5:00. The play was in Center City, so it would take about an hour to get there.

"You're gonna make me late, Drake! Where the hell have you been?" she yelled from the chair, keeping her head still to try and avoid the hot iron straightening her hair.

Kim had never been this mad before, but she was pregnant so he figured her hormones were on overdrive. All Drake could do was listen to her vent while he tried to get in the shower. Tonight, just like last night, was her night. She wanted everything to be perfect, and the only way that was going to happen was if Drake was there. She got up from the chair and headed upstairs to chew him out a little bit more, but when she got to the bedroom she couldn't find the words to speak. Her anger had been suppressed with one look at Drake in the shower. The water running down his chiseled body had her panties so wet; she was tempted to fuck up her hair by getting in the shower with him.

"I'm sorry," he said while lathering up his body with soap. "I got caught up at the bank earlier trying to open up a bank account. I waited and waited for a manager to come assist me, but he was taking too long so I left. The money is on the bed," he said, nodding his head in the direction of the 30k Veronica gave him.

Kim looked at the bed and saw that the money was there. She felt kind of bad for yelling at him when he had a good excuse for being late. Kim believed everything Drake said, even though it was mostly a lie. But he only lied because he didn't want to hurt her by telling her the truth.

"You know I love you, right?" Drake asked her as he reached for a towel while stepping out of the shower. He dried his body off as he walked past her to go into the bedroom.

"Yeah, I know you do. I just need you to spend more time with me, instead of running the streets," she said, kissing him on the lips softly and wrapping her arms around his neck.

Her lips were soft, and Drake's dick started to get hard. Kim saw the effect she was having on him. Drake wrapped his arms around her waist and pulled her closer to him, pressing her up against his naked body. She tried to push him off to get away, because she knew exactly where this was headed and she had about two hours until the play started.

"Where you going?" he asked, and kissed her, but this time swiping his tongue across her bottom lip, knowing that it would turn her on because it didn't take much for Kim to turn Drake on. In his mind, she was 5 foot 7 of pure perfection, even more so in his eyes because his seed was growing inside of her.

"No, don't do this right now. I'ma be late," she said, unable to control herself under the rapid fire of kisses Drake was sending her way.

"Ten minutes," he said, looking over at the clock and seeing that it was only 4:25.

Nothing else needed to be said, as Kim took off the robe she was wearing, leaving her in just her panties and bra, which were off before her body hit the bed. There was no time for foreplay, so Drake wasted none, sliding his large, thick, rock-hard dick inside of her wet pussy. She took a deep breath, pleasurably taking in every inch of his manhood.

As he stroked hard and deep, Kim couldn't control her cries of pleasure and whimpering. She screamed out Drake's name at the top of her lungs. With every stroke, he went deeper and deeper. The deeper he went, the wetter her pussy got.

They took turns biting and kissing each other's necks. Drake enjoyed the sensation of Kim cumming all over his dick. She begged for him to stop, but all Drake did was change positions. He flipped her body over and began hitting it from the back, spreading her legs apart so her stomach would almost touch the bed. His large hands grabbed her by the waist as he began long stroking her slowly but deeply, pushing up against the back of her vagina with his dick.

"Oh, Daddy! Oh, Daddy, go deeper! Go deeper!" she yelled out, turning her head to watch him fuck her from behind.

Deeper and harder Drake fucked Kim, making her butt cheeks clap up against his stomach. She was enjoying it so much that she had forgotten that Monica was still downstairs waiting to finish doing her hair. She bit into the pillow, bracing herself for her final orgasm that was coming on strong. She felt a tingle running through her entire body that put chill bumps all over her arms. "I'm cumming, Daddy! Oh I'm cumming, Daddy!" she yelled out.

"Cum all over Daddy's dick!" Drake shot back, pounding away and on the verge of cumming, too.

He could feel her pussy tighten up around his dick and the wetness increased, dripping off his balls and onto the bed. The feeling was like no other. Her screams turned into a soft cry.

"Cum in this pussy, Daddy!" she said, while looking back at Drake with lust-filled eyes.

Drake couldn't hold it any longer. The words she managed to get out made him cum instantly. Splashing off inside of her felt so good.

Kim could feel the warmth of his cum inside of her oozing out as Drake continued to slowly stroke, giving her every bit he had left. When he finally pulled out, it sounded like a suction cup losing its grip.

They both turned to look at the clock. It was 4:55, one hour and 25 minutes until the play started.

"I knew you were going to make me late," Kim said, stumbling to the bathroom for the quick shower she had been trying to avoid.

Drake didn't bother taking another shower. He just got dressed. Kim's cum was still covering his dick and the light sweat he had accumulated dried up when he opened one of the bedroom windows. To be honest, he could care less about being late. He'd rather stay home and fuck all night anyway.

Detective Grant walked into the office, scratching his head with a stumped look on his face. He was assigned to work the Christopher Watkins case, where a shooting took place in a lounge on the north side of Philly, leaving one dead and two others wounded. Christopher Watkins was pronounced dead at the scene with a gunshot wound to his neck. One of the victims was in Temple hospital in critical condition, fighting for his life with a bullet lodged in his chest that doctors were afraid to take out.

"I got a call last night from one of my informants who told me a woman could have been the shooter," he said to his partner, Detective Hill, while taking a seat at his desk. "A chick named Cindy from South Philly. I ran a check on the name 'Cindy', but nothing came up in the system. So whoever she is, she doesn't have a record."

"Give Codwell a call over at the Vice Unit in South Philly," Hill said, referring to Detective John Codwell in the South Philly precinct.

"Yeah, but the funny thing is that even if we could locate her, there are no witnesses or any evidence that

she was even the one who pulled the trigger, unless she still has the smoking gun somewhere in her possession. The bartender said she didn't see anything that happened because she was in the storage room grabbing more beer from the cooler. Daniel Patrick, the guy who got shot in the chest, is in critical condition, and the other guy, Robert Smith, said he doesn't know who shot him in the arm. Everybody else that was there left the scene before the uniformed cops arrived."

"Wait. Wasn't there some blood at the scene that didn't belong to any of the victims?" Hill asked, looking through the DNA evidence taken from the scene. "If there is a Cindy who was there that night, and her DNA matches what we've got, we can at least put her at the scene of the crime, and hopefully secure a warrant to search her house for a possible gun. We know from the shell casings found at the scene that it had to have been a revolver used to shoot these guys."

"But we have no motive, or any witnesses for that matter," Grant said, playing the devil's advocate. "We need more. Let's go down to the hospital and see how our friend, Daniel Patrick is doing. Hopefully by now he's out of surgery and can talk."

"What about Cindy?"

"Hell, we gotta find out who Cindy is first. I'll call John at the precinct on our way to the hospital."

Detectives Grant and Hill have worked at the 35th Precinct together for about eight years now as homicide detectives, and there hasn't been a homicide they haven't solved yet. Rookies in the police station call them the "Dream Team," because of how well they work together. Either by confession or overwhelming evidence, they

solved 47 homicide cases together, leaving the defendants who fought these cases with little to no chance for an appeal after their convictions.

Grant also had a lot of informants on the streets that worked for him, paying them with cash, and sometimes a get out of jail free card if the info they gave was important enough to pursue.

Hill, on the other hand, was excellent at piecing the puzzle together. He took the evidence, analyzed it for hours—sometimes days—and then he'd come up with a scenario of how a murder had taken place.

Never once in their careers did either of the detectives falsify evidence or force any witnesses to testify. They didn't have to. They were that good.

One thing for sure was that they were gathering all the information they could in this case, and Cindy's name was the first thing they were going to figure out, after seeing if Daniel Patrick made it through the night. Daniel had flatlined twice on the operating table, so it wasn't looking too good for him. If he did regain consciousness, he probably wouldn't remember who had shot him anyway, let alone the events that happened that night. Robert Smith wasn't cooperating at all, so Daniel was probably their only chance of solving this case.

Chapter 5

It was Friday, and Cindy left the hospital early that morning, still in pain but not willing to stick around in case the cops came back to ask a couple more questions. It was standard hospital policy to inform the police of any patient with a gunshot wound and have a report filed.

When the police came to question Cindy, she had told them she was just walking down the street, and a guy tried to rob her. When she refused to give him any money, he shot her. Knowing that story wasn't going to hold up very long, she checked out of the hospital under the fake name she gave.

"I got to get back up and running again," Cindy told D-Rock, as she walked into the living room of her house, eating ice cream. "I lost a lot of money in the past week, and I know all my customers had to buy their shit from somebody else."

"I know, but you got to get some rest. You need to let ya wounds heal properly," D-Rock said out of concern.

"Fuck my wounds, D-Rock. I need money. These high ass bills can't get paid wit' my smile. I got a lot of people out there struggling right now, and the one thing I refuse to do is leave my young soldiers hungry," she told him while picking up her cell phone.

"You know you got beef in the streets now. You can't just kill somebody and think that person's family won't want some type of revenge."

"Beef comes with the game, D-Rock," she said without a care in the world, and then acknowledged the person on the other end of the phone. "Hello, I would like to place an order."

"Yeah, what can I get you?"

"I would like ten pieces of chicken, two small fries and a large Pepsi."

"Is that a pick-up or a delivery?" the man asked.

"Delivery, and could you make it fast because I'm hungry as hell!" Cindy said in a serious voice. "It's Ms. C. I order from there all the time, so y'all already got my address. Call me back when the food is done cooking," she said, then hung up the phone.

D-Rock looked at her and couldn't help but to chuckle a bit. Cindy reminded him so much of her father, who was his best friend. She acted just like him in every way imaginable, and her strong fearless attitude showed it all. She kind of looks like him too, he thought to himself, chuckling a little more.

After Cindy got off her phone call for some reason her mind switched to thinking about the man who saved her life. The one thing she couldn't figure out was why Drake helped her. She was thankful for everything that he did, but it was just that good people like him were hard to come by when it came to the lifestyle she lived. He was even kind of cute, she thought to herself, changing channels on the TV to see if anything good was on.

"Look, I know you're going to do whatever you want, Cindy, but I just want you to be careful out there in these streets. I don't want to have to come out of retirement, but you know I will."

Cindy was in a zone. She didn't hear a word D-Rock was saying. All she could think about was how she planned to get her street corners up and running again. Beef with whoever felt some type of way about Chris' death meant nothing to her. Whatever was going to happen, it was going to happen. But in the meantime, money was on her mind... that, and Drake.

Drake woke up to the smell of sausages, eggs and toast burning in the kitchen, making his stomach growl instantly. The play had been a hit last night, and even though Kim had been late, she made it in time to perform her part and she killed it. Monica, on the other hand, kept her eyes on Drake all night, thinking about how he had made Kim scream the way she did before they went to the play. She couldn't help but wonder if he could have her screaming his name the same way.

When Drake looked over at his phone, he saw that he had 17 missed calls, all from Veronica. He had forgotten that he told her to call him last night. If she called this many times, it had to be something important, so he called her back. Her phone rang twice before she answered it.

"Nigga, where the hell have you been? I been tryin' to call you all night and this morning."

"I had to take care of something with Kim last night."

"Yeah, I know. Kim told me this morning."

"What? Kim told you this morning?" He was shocked at the fact she and Kim were actually talking.

A few months ago, Kim thought Drake was fucking Veronica, so she stepped to Veronica, strapped with a gun. In the end, Kim told her to stay away from Drake, and if she ever caught them together, she was going to shoot her in the face. She wasn't serious. She just wanted to scare the shit out of Veronica.

It was even more surprising to Drake that as he was talking to Veronica on his way downstairs, she was sitting in the kitchen eating breakfast with Kim. He was unaware that she reached out to Kim a while ago; they had called a truce and were now cool.

Kim and Veronica shared a quick laugh before Drake sat down at the table, and then Kim got up and went upstairs, leaving Drake and Veronica alone.

"What's goin' on, V?" Drake asked, wondering why she was sitting in his kitchen.

"Look, I found a way that we could take a lot more money out of Tazz's account. I don't know if I told you about my girlfriend, but she's a computer geek and she gave me the game."

"What's the game, V?"

"The only way Christine could have access to whatever she wants in that account is if both parties agree to it. Tazz doesn't even have to be there to do it. The bank would call Tazz over the phone if he couldn't make it down there, and ask him a few personal questions to make sure that he was the right person. After that, both parties can agree on the amount of money that was accessible."

"How the hell are we supposed to do that?"

"All we need is a cell phone that's untraceable, and someone to memorize all of Tazz's personal information. That's where you come in," she told him, passing him an envelope with all of Tazz's personal info in it.

"How are they going to call me? I don't even have the phone yet."

Veronica pulled out a Boost Mobil cell phone and passed it to him. She was well prepared from the time she woke up this morning. Patricia had provided her with all of Tazz's personal information that Drake needed. Patricia was an animal with the internet. She could get anybody's personal account numbers, Social Security numbers, PIN numbers, dates of birth, and all other pertinent information you could think of. There wasn't much you could hide from her.

"So, after we change the access amount, what happens next?" Drake asked.

"Well, this is where it gets a little complicated. First, we are going to make the account an open account so there's no limit or restrictions to how much money we can take out. It won't be safe for us to keep withdrawing large amounts of money, so we should take it all in two shots. After the account is open, I'm going to transfer $1.8 million in an offshore account under a different name, and then another $2.5 million into another offshore account."

"Where is this money supposed to be, and how are we going to get access to the money after it's in another bank?" Drake wanted to know.

"For 100k, Patricia has a friend in Brazil that will exchange Brazilian money for American money. She said that whenever we're ready, she'd make the phone call. The second transfer, which will be the $1.8 million—my cut— will be transferred to a Swiss account. It will be transferred several times before it comes back to the United States."

"How long is this process supposed to take?" Drake was now frustrated and tapping the envelope on the table.

"Think of it as taking a vacation. Brazil is a hot spot this time of the year. One week and you'll be $2.5 million richer. And the best part about it is that you'll be someone other than yourself. I have to meet up with Patricia later on to get your new identification for when you get there. But before we do anything, I have to get to the bank this morning so we can make the changes with the account."

"Veronica," he said in a concerned manner, getting her attention. "Is this the only way we can get this money out of his account?"

"No. We can keep taking 100k a day for the next several days until they find out the money is missing. That's a lot of running around to do every day. I think we've got a better chance at taking a large lump sum, and then doing it the way I plan to. But the choice is yours. You are the boss."

Drake sat in silence and thought about it for a minute, weighing the good and the possible bad qualities. Two-point-five million dollars was a nice piece of money for a week's worth of work, and if all went well, this could be a robbery nobody would have to die in. Then he thought about the plan not working, and if they got caught trying to steal Tazz's money. Jail time would be the least of his problems if Tazz got a hold of him after he got out of jail. Fuck it! It is what it is, he thought to himself.

"I think you should be on your way to the bank, Mrs. Fields, if we're going to make this happen. I'll keep the phone on and have Tazz's info handy. Remember, if anything goes wrong or even looks funny in that bank, you drop everything and keep it movin'."

Drake really didn't have to tell Veronica what to do if anything went wrong at the bank, because she was well aware of security matters, and how long procedures like this are supposed to take. The bottom line; she was damn near an expert at what she did, probably the best in the city for that matter, not to mention that she had a powerhouse computer geek for a friend who loved gifts from Tiffany's.

The deliveryman showed up in less than twenty minutes, pulling into Cindy's driveway and getting out with two bags. Max's Pizza was really just a front for selling cocaine, and Maximus Garcia was at the head of the operation. He had six delivery cars, including two bike boys that would deliver anywhere from 4 ½ ounces to 20 bricks of cocaine.

In order to place an order for cocaine, you had to know the right thing to say. Max's only made pizza, so if you asked for chicken wings, one chicken wing was equal to one brick of cocaine. French fries were bake, and a large Pepsi meant just what it was: a large Pepsi. Cooking cocaine can make you thirsty sometimes.

Cindy got the coke and went straight to the kitchen, pulling out a large Pyrex pot from the cabinet. Her whip game was vicious. It was easy for her to drop a whole brick in the pot and cook it to the oils, but she recently learned a new method of slow cooking cocaine, which almost doubled the product without losing the quality of its purity.

Cooking only 18 ounces at a time gave Cindy the opportunity to blend the cut into the cocaine more effectively. For every 18 ounces of cocaine, she brought back 26 to 27 ounces of crack, depending on how good the cocaine was before cooking it. When the crack became hard and dried up on the plate, she broke it down into quarter ounces, half ounces, and whole ounces for the clientele she had with weight sales.

She was in the kitchen all day, cooking cocaine with a bullet wound in her stomach. She was hungry with the vision of money clouding her brain. Phone calls were made to all of her workers to let them know that she was back in business.

It would take another day or two to bag up the crack for street sales, and that process in itself was the hardest, especially when you break down whole bricks into ten-dollar rocks. That was more than just a process; it was a three shift job that cramped up every finger on your hands from opening the 5/8 super small baggies for hours. It was a good thing that Cindy had a team just for that job, and she paid them well.

Chapter 6

Villain drove to New York to make the deal with Blue Black. He brought along Rick, one of his bodyguards who loved to shoot. He would kill anything that could bleed, and if it wouldn't bleed, he would surely use every bullet he had to make it do so. This wasn't the first time Villain had dealt with Blue, but with twenty bricks involved, everybody was on their P's and Q's.

Blue, in a dark blue Cadillac truck with tinted windows, pulled into the parking lot across from the Four Seasons hotel where they were supposed to meet. There were only about 7 to 10 more cars on the third level when he pulled in to see that Villain was already there, sitting on the hood of a Dodge Charger and smoking a cigarette. Rick stood to the side, holding a Mac 90 in plain sight for everyone to see.

"The head honcho, Villain! What's crackin', playa?" Blue said, walking over to Villain and taking a seat on the car with him. "Talk to big homie. What's the mathematics?" he said, referring to how much the coke was going to cost.

"Prices went up, Blue. I need twenty grand a brick this time around, and I can't take no shorts."

Blue remained calm, trying not to get angry at the fact that he was just paying 17.5 a brick and the prices went up this high so fast. It was Villain who shot the price up this high in the first place because Tazz told him to only charge Blue 18.5. When Tazz sets a price, it doesn't change under any circumstances unless Tazz changes it himself. This was something that Villain knew, but he never seemed to follow the rules, which Tazz was unaware of.

"Damn, playa! Twenty-k?" he asked, shocked at the price. "At least let me see what you got. If I gotta spend 20k a brick, I gotta see what I'm buying first. Plus, I'ma have to go and get the rest of the money you're asking for, because I only brought 350k. I'm short like twenty grand.

Villain took him to the trunk of the car and pulled out a green duffel bag with the coke in it. Blue opened the bag and examined the contents for a minute, and then agreed to the price, with the exception that he could owe the other 20k and pay it in a couple days. Villain denied the request and demanded that he pay it all right now, either that or just buy 19 bricks instead of 20.

The conversation was interrupted by two cars that pulled onto the 3rd level and stopped directly in front of the Dodge Charger.

The attention the two cars got from Villain and Rick gave Blue enough time to pull out a black .357 Sig Sauer from his waistband and point it in the direction of Villain's head. What started as a drug deal became a robbery in less than five minutes and out of the two cars came four of Blue's boys carrying large semi-automatic handguns. One of them even had an AR-15.

"You know what this is, old boy," Blue said, walking up close to Villain and taking his gun from his waistband.

Rick wanted so badly to set it off and fire the first bullet into Blue's face, but the occupants from the cars had already begun to spread out to circle the Charger, limiting Rick's target to one person. If he were to shoot, it would have been suicide.

"It ain't nothin' personal, just business. Now, the decision you gotta make is if you want to walk out of this parking lot, or roll out of this motherfucker. If you roll out, you'll roll out in a body bag," Blue said, waving his gun around.

Villain didn't think Blue was going to let him leave the parking lot alive, but he really didn't have much of a choice but to comply. The coke could be replaced, but his life could not. Nor could Rick's.

Blue told Rick to pop the clip out of his gun and take the bullet out of the chamber. Rick looked at Blue like he was crazy. He wasn't willing or ready to disarm himself.

Not wanting to, Villain spoke up and told Rick to do what Blue said, trying to give them a better chance at making it out alive. Blue really didn't want to kill Villain, but he would if Rick acted like he wanted to shoot it out.

Rick eventually complied, throwing the clip on the ground and taking the bullet out of the chamber. With that being done, Blue directed one of his boys to get the coke out of the trunk, along with the gun that Rick had.

What Blue did next would put the icing on the cake. He made Rick and Villain strip down to their boxers, took the car keys from Villain and made them walk out of the parking lot. "Don't bring ya bitch asses back to New York," he told Villain, kicking him in the ass while he was walking away.

Blue and his boys laughed the entire time while putting the coke in the car and watching Villain and Rick walk out of the parking lot.

There were no words that could explain the way Villain felt. One thing for certain was that Blue started a war, and Villain wouldn't stop until he killed him, or Blue killed Villain first.

The plan worked out well. The bank called the cell phone just like Veronica said they would, and Drake answered every question correctly and swiftly, as though he was Tazz. The money was on its way to the Cayman Islands. The next thing was getting it from the Caymans to Mexico, and then into the United States. That was the only way the money could make it back into the States in cash form. Recently, the United States government cracked down on U.S. citizens putting money in offshore accounts to avoid taxes, so it was hard avoiding the government.

Veronica booked the next flight to the Cayman Islands, which would be leaving Saturday morning. They would be staying at the Renaissance Hotel for four days and three nights, which was enough time to pick up the cash from the bank on Monday. Veronica called the bank and scheduled the cash withdrawal of $2.5 million in U.S. currency. She transferred the money into an account under another identity. The $1.8 million was transferred into a Swiss account that Veronica planned to withdraw at a later date, pending the outcome of the $2.5 million making it back to the States.

The new identities for Drake and Veronica were perfect. They both had their game faces on for the trip.

Everything was going well as more celebrities showed up to Tazz's club and soon the place was packed. At the center of everything was Peaches, dressed in a plunging Gucci white silk crepe mini dress, a pair of super high strappy sandals, and white gold and sapphire panther-shaped stud earrings. She looked stunning, and by all the attention she was receiving, she knew it.

It had been a while since Peaches hit the club scene or any kind of social event with celebrities, mostly due to the relationship she had with Drake. Even though they had an open relationship, she still considered herself to be his girl, and for that reason alone she never cheated on him.

"Yo, mama, I need to holla at you for a second," Tazz yelled out over the music to Peaches. "Follow me," he said, pulling her away from the crowd that was hovering around her. Damn! Everybody is feelin' shawty, he thought to himself as he made his way through the crowd with Peaches close behind him.

Instead of hosting one of the local celebrity rappers, Tazz had her host the NBA players when he found out they were coming. To her surprise, Peaches was having a blast, partying, drinking, dancing, and getting a lot of attention from all sorts of good-looking men. She hadn't had this much fun in months, and she loved it.

"Have a seat," Tazz said, entering his office, which was was located on the second floor of the club. "You know, the people like you here. You're bringing a new vibe to the club that I haven't seen since I opened the place. It's crazy because it's only your first night."

"Well, I'm just having fun." Peaches smiled.

"Look, what if I asked you to work for me full time; eight hours a day, four days a week, including a couple holidays? I also wanna give you a higher position so you can make more money. I was thinking about making you the assistant manager. You'll take care of all the dancers, plan parties, and assign hosts to our customers."

Peaches sat back in the chair and looked out of the window at the people dancing in the middle of the club and imagining what it would be like to do something like that as a job. She never really had a job before. She was so beautiful that whatever man she was with spoiled her with everything she wanted… everyone but Drake. He gave her money and treated her well, but he was doing the same thing with Kim.

Tazz threw a wad of money on the table. "This is three thousand dollars for working tonight and tomorrow. Tell me what it's going to cost me to keep you."

Peaches grabbed the money and put it into her bag, thinking to herself that this was the easiest three grand she had ever made. For a moment, she had truly forgotten about the reason she was there in the first place. She was there for Drake, and that's where her loyalty lay. The offer was good and it was almost impossible to turn down, especially with Tazz's charming smile lighting up the room.

Before she could even answer Tazz, Villain came running into the room with fury in his eyes and kicked Peaches out immediately. He didn't have to tell her twice, because by the time he got to the end of, "Get the fuck out!" she had already made her exit.

"Calm down, nigga! What the fuck is goin' on?" Tazz yelled at Villain. He was so angry that he just killed the mood in the room.

"Da muthafucka, Blue, robbed me for the twenty bricks! Da nigga set me up!"

Tazz looked at Villain with disgust. For as long as Villain has been selling drugs with Tazz, neither one of them had ever been robbed. There were a few attempts, but none was ever successful. It bothered Tazz that his first instinct was that Villain was lying because he had a lot of trust in him. But he also knew that Villain secretly snorted cocaine.

"I'ma kill that muthafucka! I'ma kill that muthafucka!" Villain yelled as he angrily paced around the room.

"Listen. Sit and calm down. You runnin' around my office like a madman ain't helping no one, and it damn sure ain't bringing my cocaine back." Tazz picked up the office phone, dialed a number, and waited for the phone to start ringing.

"Yo, who the hell is this?" Blue answered.

"Damn, Blue. You into robberies now?" Tazz calmly spoke into the phone as though the 20 bricks didn't mean a thing.

"You know, Tazz, I would like to chat wit' you, but I'm sure the beef is on between me and you. I'm getting my money right so the war we're gonna have can be fun."

"War? You think it's goin' to be a war? I'm not goin' to war wit' you, Blue. Flat out, I'ma kill you, and anybody else who say they love you."

"Bitch ass nigga, you Philly niggas is soft. Come holla at me, playboy. You know where I'm at," Blue said, and then hung up the phone.

Tazz was mad as hell, but he didn't show it to Villain. "We got the deal for the 200 keys coming up Monday morning. Before we take care of Blue, I want to get my drugs first. I'm giving you the green light to do whatever you want to do, just as long as it's after the deal. Right now, I want you to go home and chill out. We can't get nothing done wit' you mad like this. I give you my word, Blue won't be able to enjoy any of that money."

Detectives Hill and Grant had been back and forth to the hospital all week, hoping that Daniel would come out of his coma and be able to tell them who shot him. Today, he finally awoke, but was in and out of consciousness. Hill was the only one at his bedside while Grant had been going through South Philly to see if anyone knew who Cindy was.

Nobody really talks to the cops in South Philly except for the informants that the police have everywhere. But even so, there weren't too many people who didn't like Cindy in the hood. She looked out for a lot of people and had done some good things for the neighborhood. So the fact that she sold drugs was overlooked by many, and to turn her over to the cops could take a lifetime.

"Who shot you?" Detective Hill asked Daniel when his eyes opened. "Who did this to you?"

Daniel's mouth was so dry that he couldn't even talk. You could hear heavy breathing, but words couldn't come out of his mouth. The bullet was still lodged in his chest, and the doctors didn't want to take any chances going back in to try and retrieve it because he had already flatlined twice on the operating table. His transfer to another hospital was one signature away, due to the fact that Temple Hospital's doctors weren't capable of doing anything else for him.

"My name is Detective Hill. Can you talk? Who shot you? You might die, son! I'm trying to find out who did this to you!" Hill yelled.

"Girl... girl..." Daniel managed to whisper before he fell unconscious again.

In the field of law enforcement sometimes you had to be patient, and patience is what Hill had, even if he had to visit the next hospital that Daniel was transferred to. Grant, on the other hand, was getting frustrated at the neighborhood for not helping him out. It was so bad that he almost ran into a truck coming down 23rd Street. He'd been working the case day and night without much rest in between. This was the way he and his partner did things—trying their best to get as much info as they could within the first seventy-two hours. This was part of the reason why they were the best.

Chapter 7

It was pouring in the Caymans when Drake and Veronica arrived there on Saturday morning. Being as discrete as possible, they checked into the hotel where they had reserved two separate rooms.

Sleeping separately was Veronica's idea, because she wanted to avoid all the temptations of doing something they both might regret. Growing up, she never looked at Drake as boyfriend material, but as they got older things changed. Mainly Drake had gone from a boy to a fully well-developed man, leaving a bit of curiosity on Veronica's part. It was only out of respect for Kim that she never stepped to Drake.

Drake walked out of the bathroom to answer his phone. It hadn't stopped ringing while he was in the shower. He was trying to get cleaned up before he and Veronica went to get something to eat at one of the local restaurants. It was Peaches calling. He hadn't spoken to her since Thursday.

"What's good, baby girl," he answered, happy that she had called.

"Damn, Drake! Where the hell are you, and why the hell aren't you answering your phone?" she said with an attitude.

"Slow down, ma. I'm in the Caymans right now. I'm out here taking care of some business. Why? What's going on?"

"Who are you in the Caymans with?"

"A friend. I'll be back in a couple days."

Peaches was getting angrier with every word Drake spoke. He's probably out there wit' some chick, she was thinking to herself and wondering what kind of business he had to conduct that took him to the Caymans.

Drake never had time to call her and tell her about Veronica's plan to steal Tazz's money, which left Peaches thinking that Drake was vacationing without her.

"Well, I was calling you because I had some good news I thought you might wanna hear."

"Well, tell me."

"I was at Tazz's club last night hosting a party..."

Drake cut her off in the middle of what she was about to say. "What the hell do you mean, you was hosting a party at Tazz's club!"

"Just shut up and listen to me. I was sitting in his office being offered a job, when all of a sudden one of his boys came storming in, kicking me out, yelling and screaming at the top of his lungs to Tazz. I sat outside the door and listened to their conversation about how the guy had got robbed earlier yesterday. But that's not all! I heard Tazz and the other guy talking about a shipment

53

of cocaine they have to pick up next week. Two-hundred bricks, papi!" she said with excitement.

There was a moment of silence over the phone before Drake spoke another word. "Two hundred bricks?" he asked, making sure that he heard Peaches right.

"Yeah, and the deal is going down Monday morning. I think the shipment is going to the club, but I'm not sure."

Two hundred keys of cocaine was a lot of coke, and it sent a chill down Drake's spine just thinking about it. He was almost upset because he was stuck in the Caymans for the next few days... until Veronica walked through the door. She was wearing a black lace, sleeveless dress with a sexy sheer underlay. It almost gave the illusion that she was naked. Her ample breasts and every single curve seemed to be in 3D.

Although many would consider Veronica to be a striking woman, Drake never checked for her on some sexual attraction shit. But the way she was looking at him with that smile on her face, highlighting her dimples and seductive eyes had him questioning that. Flawless was the only word that could describe her, and it took a business trip to the Cayman Islands for Drake to see how beautiful she was.

It was hard for him to continue his phone conversation with Peaches while Veronica was standing in front of him. "Look, just keep ya eyes on him until I get back to the city," he told Peaches, and then hung up the phone. "Damn, V! You lookin' good! How I'm supposed to go out wit' you tonight?" he joked, really just complimenting her on how good she looked. Something he never really did, but they didn't have that sort of relationship and honestly, he preferred to keep it that way.

"I've got money, so I think I should at least dress like it," she said with a smile.

"I feel you. Let me get ready so we can go."

Drake took his time getting dressed, and Veronica couldn't help but to notice how sexy he looked without his shirt on. His well-muscled chest that had tattoos all over it and chiseled stomach had Veronica staring at him with greed in her eyes. She felt her lust getting the best of her and tried to calm it down. Veronica had no panties on and caught herself having visions of Drake lifting her dress and having his way with her. She would have loved for it to happen, but he did not seem interested.

Dinner was even more awkward for Veronica when the waiter treated them as if they were a couple, providing champagne and candles at a table where the lighting was dim and the mood was on the romantic side. Drake, dressed like a thug, wearing a white T-shirt, jeans and sneakers, caused the people around them to wonder why such a well-dressed Veronica would be interested in a man like that. If they only knew the history between the two of them, they would completely understand.

Cindy's first couple of days back rolling around the South Philly streets was kind of funny. A lot of people were happy to see her Range Rover coming down the street, especially her workers. The money had slowed up for a while, but she knew just how to get business back booming. To practically give away the cocaine by making her crack bags the largest the city ever had. She had to get her clientele back up, so she made sacrifices she knew would pay off.

Twenty-third Street was the first strip she paid close attention to. There was still a lot of tension in the air about Chris getting killed, and a few death threats were passed on to a couple of her workers.

Her bullet wound was healing pretty well, but she was still a little cautious about walking around too much. So when she pulled up, she stayed inside the car and talked to her worker, Little Rick, about the word on the streets. Not only was Little Rick her best worker, but he also was her eyes and ears on the street when she wasn't around. Someone like Cindy needed that kind of person for times like this.

"What's the word out here, Rick?" she asked after rolling down the window and sitting back in her seat like the boss that she was.

His name was Little Rick, but he wasn't little at all. In fact, Little Rick was rather large, being 6-ft. 1-in. and 245 lbs. solid. They only call him Little Rick because he's the smallest in his family. He pushed a lot of weight for Cindy ever since she took over South Philly, and at the age of 26, he had about 13 years in the drug game. He didn't fear Cindy or look at her differently because she was a woman deep in the drug game. But rather, he respected her ambition to make money and do it her way.

"Yo, the detectives been coming around here asking about who you were and where they could find you at," Rick informed her, looking up and down the street at the flow of traffic. "They didn't flash any pictures, so I'm guessing they don't know what you look like."

"Yeah? So what's going on with 9th Street?" she asked, not seeming to care too much about the detectives. "Did you hear anything about Chris' people?"

"Nah, but the funeral is tomorrow. I didn't hear it personally, but the word is that they know who killed him. I think you should stay low for a while until things die down. Don't worry about the block. I'll take care of all ya' footwork if you need me to."

"Thanks, Rick, but I'm not ducking. If they wanna see me, then let them come. It'll just be a bunch of funerals and a sad year for South Philly," she said, taking the chrome .45 out of her center console. "I think it's about time we start moving our business beyond 15th Street."

Fifteenth Street on down was Chris' neighborhood. He ran that part of South Philly, and they got just as much, if not more money, than the part of South Philly Cindy ran. Now that Chris was gone, his turf was open to the highest bidder, and Cindy wanted to stake her claim. In fact, she wanted all of it; the whole South Philly, and there was pretty much nobody big enough to stop her.

Blue was poppin' bottles of Ace all night at the night club, courtesy of Villain. That wasn't the only thing that was poppin' though. One hundred and thirty-first and Rockaway on the south side of Jamaica, Queens had stepped up to a whole other level, considering the fact that Blue never scored this much cocaine in his life. He wasn't broke, but

20 keys was a bit out of his league. With the little extra money he was making, he was spending it just as fast as he was making it.

He went to the dealership and bought a brand new S550 Benz, fully loaded with custom tinted windows, and a pair of 20-inch Giovanni rims, easily spending 100k for one car.

It didn't cause too much of a dent in his pockets because he broke down 15 out of the 20 keys he took from Villain. From each brick of cocaine he turned into crack, he produced 55 ounces, making $1500 off of each ounce, minus two to three hundred per ounce for crack-heads that spend a lot of money and expect a deal for what they're paying for.

"So, what you gonna do about that nigga, Villain?" one of Blue's boys asked while they were sitting in VIP.

"Fuck Villain! I'll see him when I see him. If he comes back to NYC wit' that bullshit, I'ma blow his muthafuckin' head off. You worrying about the wrong shit right now. Try worrying about taking one of these bitches home wit' you tonight," he told his boy, pointing at the two women dancing on the couches in front of them.

Deep down inside, Blue was thinking about how he should have killed Villain in that parking lot instead of just letting him go with a bruised ass from the Timberland boot he kicked him with. It was a guarantee that Villain was coming for those 20 bricks, and more. Blue was sure that he wanted blood, too. What man wouldn't want blood after being humiliated, robbed, and then kicked in the ass?

"Yo, I want you to tell everybody to be on high alert. There shouldn't be anybody standing outside without a gun from now on," Blue told his boy. "If anybody sees Villain before I do, blast his ass and whoever else is with him."

Kim was getting worried about Drake because she hadn't heard from him all weekend. The last time she saw him was the morning that Veronica stopped by the house.

Not only was Kim worried, she was also getting fed up with Drake's bullshit. Staying out all night and not coming home until late the next day was taking a toll on her. The fucked up part about it was that she remained faithful to him even though she knew he was fucking other women. Kim loved him for about two years now, and deep down inside she knew that he loved her back. But she also knew about Peaches for about a few months now.

Up until about two months ago, Drake was being a good man in Kim's eyes, and if he was sleeping around he didn't show it. But now, the signs were slapping her all up in her face, plus she was pregnant with his child. He was about to be a father. It was time to take off the gloves. She dialed Drake's phone and he didn't answer, but that didn't stop her from calling him right back. She was determined to talk to him. If Drake thought she was going to let up from calling him this early in the morning, he had another thing coming. She called back to back to back to back to back until Drake finally answered.

"What's up, babe?" he asked after being awoken by the phone's consistent ringing in his ear.

"Is there a reason why you been out since Friday and you haven't called here to let me know what's going on? I've been worried sick about you. Where the hell are you?" Kim asked with an attitude that she felt she had the right to have.

"I'm sorry, Kim. I should have called you, but I was caught up wit' trying to take care of my business."

"Where are you, Drake?" she interrupted, after he didn't answer the question the first time.

There was a brief silence before Drake answered. "I'm in the Caymans."

"The Caymans!" Kim snapped. "What the hell are you doing in the Caymans? As a matter of fact, who are you there with?"

Once again, silence lingered over the phone. Drake didn't want to lie to her, but he knew that the truth was not what she really wanted to hear right now. He loved her enough to protect her heart; although he didn't realize she did not need such protection. She just wanted the truth. "I came out here wit' my man, Bones. We got some business out here that I can't explain over the phone. I'll explain everything when I get home."

"Yo' man, Bones?" she asked, not believing a word he just said. Keeping Drake on the line, she picked up the house phone and dialed Veronica's cell phone number.

Drake, seeing that Kim had called him from her cell phone, didn't realize what she was up to until the sounds of Veronica's phone lit up the room like fireworks on the 4th of July, bringing another round of silence over the phone.

"Are you going to answer the phone, or is Veronica gonna play like she's not there with you?" Kim asked sarcastically.

Drake's face went blank for a moment before smiling at Kim's cleverness. Being caught in a lie was the worst feeling he could feel, especially being caught by Kim.

Veronica couldn't help but to smile too. That was something that she would do if the shoe were on the other foot. But at the same time she felt bad for Kim, because she probably thought that she and Drake were sleeping together, which wasn't the case by far.

"Kim, it's not what you think. Me and…"

Kim hung up the phone in Drake's ear before he could get another lie out. Knowing Drake would try to call her back; she turned off her cell phone and took the house phone off of the hook. She didn't want to be bothered by him or his lies right now.

"Why didn't you just tell her the truth, stupid?" Veronica said, throwing a pillow at his head. "Now you got that girl all upset and thinking that we're out here doing something. I swear, if she pulls another gun out on me, I'ma fuck you up!" she said jokingly, but also very serious. "You're stupid!" she said again, throwing another pillow at Drake.

Chapter 8

Everything was going well with Cindy. Most of her crack houses were up and running and her side of South Philly was active again. She came to meet up with Rick to make sure all was good on his end.

Rick pulled himself away from the heavy flow of traffic going into the crack house when he saw Cindy get out of the truck. He had known her for a few years now, and every time Rick was in her presence, he felt the urge to tell her how he really felt about her. He had love for Cindy as a friend and a business partner in the beginning, but as time went on, his feelings ran much deeper. The only thing that stopped him from telling her how he felt was the fact that he was working for her, and he thought maybe she might have looked down on him to a certain extent.

"What's good wit' you?" he asked Cindy, while leaning up against the truck and not taking his eyes off of all the movement going up around them.

"I got something big coming up in a few days, Rick. I need you," she said, taking off her sunglasses, staring in the same direction he was.

Just the sound of Cindy's voice and how she said she needed him was enough to get him to do just about anything for her. He took his eyes off the traffic for a moment to look at her. She seemed sincere. Whatever she was talking about sounded serious, he thought to himself. "Whatever you need, I got you," he said, turning his attention to a blue car with tinted windows turning down the block.

The car stopped at the corner of the block for a couple of seconds before slowly making its way down the street. It stopped again, and this time a man got out of the passenger side and crossed over to the same side of the street Cindy and Rick were on.

Instinctively, Rick drew a .45 cal. automatic from his waistband, grabbed Cindy by her waist and cuffed her behind him. She didn't even realize what was going on until she looked to see the guy walking down the street and pulling out a large caliber automatic handgun from out of his back pocket. Before she could ask Rick what was going on, shots began to ring out.

Friends that were walking down the street began to scatter and take cover behind parked cars. The rain of bullets forced Rick and Cindy to take cover behind Cindy's truck, turning it into a shield. Cindy wanted so badly to get to her gun that was under the driver's seat so she could give Rick some assistance in shooting back.

Rick waited patiently until the hail of bullets silenced, hoping that by the time he lifted his head from behind the truck, he could catch the guy trying to reload. What really happened was even better. He picked his head up just in time to see the guy jumping back into the car, which had to drive past the Range Rover in order to get off that street. As the car sped down the street, Rick opened fire at the driver's side window as it passed by. Several bullets ripped through the window, hitting the driver in the chest and causing him to swerve out of control and crash into a parked car.

Cindy immediately went for her gun while Rick hesitated to approach the car that had another guy in the passenger seat. As he got closer, shots coming from the car made him back off. Although the driver was dead, the passenger continued to fire his weapon despite the fact he couldn't get out of the car due to his door being pinned against the parked car they had crashed into.

Cindy, being fearless, walked up to the car from the rear and began firing shots through the back window, hitting the passenger in the back of his head. She acted fast, walking up to the driver's door, opening it and firing two more shots into the lifeless bodies of the two men.

"I knew that dude," Rick said about the driver as he walked up to the car. "That's one of Chris' boys. He came through here with Chris before."

"Get in my car and follow me," Cindy said, pushing the driver over on the passenger side, and then getting behind the wheel.

Rick ran back to the riddled truck and pulled up behind the car Cindy managed to get started and operable. She pulled off, turning down Dickerson Street, being careful of what she touched while driving, considering the fact she had two dead bodies in the car. She could hear her phone ringing and when she grabbed it from her waist she could see that it was Rick calling. "You still behind me?" she asked, answering the phone and looking into the rear view mirror.

"Yeah, but where the fuck are you going?" he asked, concerned that the police might show up any minute now.

"We got to make a statement. If we don't, Chris' boys are going to keep coming through my hood shooting up everything, and I can't go for that," Cindy answered, looking over at the two dead bodies. "Just stay behind me."

Cindy pulled up to 13th Street where Chris used to hang out, and saw that there were a lot of people outside; mostly drug dealers and crackheads. It was midday and the sun was shining bright. Music was blasting in the air, cars were being washed and at the end of the street, there was a dice game going on that seemed to attract a lot of people. Cindy was about to put an end to this beautiful, sunny afternoon.

She stopped the car at the end of block and got out, pulled the dead driver back into the driver's seat and put his feet on the gas, revving the car while it was still in park.

Crackheads were walking by and slowing down to see what was going on, and the guys who were sitting in the middle of the block also glanced up the street, trying to figure out what was slowing up traffic.

Taking some tissue from out of the center console, Cindy wiped down the steering wheel and the door handle as quickly as she could, because her being there started to draw attention. With the driver's side window shot out and the door closed, she reached inside and threw the gear into drive and watched the car roll down the street. She then jumped into the truck that Rick had double-parked on Christian Street and it was deuces to them motherfuckers.

Chapter 9

Peaches cracked her eyes open, only to be shocked at the sight of Tazz lying next to her. The pain from the swelling of her vagina told the story of what happened last night. Visions of Tazz on top of her, digging his dick deep within her womb flashed in and out of her mind as she slowly got out of the bed and headed for the bathroom. How the fuck did I get here? She asked herself while looking in the mirror at all the passion marks on her neck.

The first person that came to her mind was Drake, and her eyes started to fill with tears at the thought of cheating on him.

"You good in there?" Tazz asked from the bedroom, finally waking up from his deep sleep.

His voice sent a chill through Peaches' heart while she sat on the toilet to examine her vagina. "Yeah, I'm good," she shot back.

She came out of the bathroom, rushing to get her clothes that were thrown all over the place.

Tazz grabbed a hold of her arm when she tried to breeze past him. He could see the worry in her eyes and the regret all over her face. "Hold up for a second. Look at me," he said, trying to get her attention and holding her in front of him. They stood there in the middle of the bedroom, naked and looking at each other.

When Peaches got a good look at Tazz, more visions of last night flashed in her head, and him standing there naked wasn't making things any better. A crazy feeling of being turned on by his ripped body confused her, and for a moment Peaches could see how she ended up having sex with him. But last night was a blur, considering all the Ace of Spades she drank at the club, the only thing she could remember was clips of Tazz fucking the shit out of her, literally.

"You runnin' out of here like you got somewhere to go. Did I do something wrong?" Tazz asked, gently holding her by the arm.

"I don't even remember how I got here last night," she admitted, confused about this whole ordeal. "I don't even know where I am! Shit!" she yelled out. "Did we use a condom?" she asked with a concerned look on her face, praying that they at least did that part right.

Tazz was starting to feel bad because he really thought for a moment that he and Peaches had a connection. They had dinner after the party at the club last night, and they talked about their goals for the future. They even talked about how Tazz was going to end up leaving his wife because she was stealing from him. "Damn, Peaches! You don't remember nothing that happened last night?" he asked, pulling her closer to him.

She wanted to pull away from him, but for some odd reason it felt kind of good to be this intimate with someone other than Drake. This odd feeling she was having also made her remember a few things that went on last night besides sex. The events that took place came rushing back to her so much that she had to sit down on the bed. She couldn't help but to notice the size of Tazz's dick as he reached down to grab his boxers off the floor, and from the looks of it she could see why she felt the way she did.

"Look, I guess we both had a little too much to drink," he said, sitting down next to her on the bed. "I apologize if you did something you didn't want to do last night. And for the record, I want you to know that I really do like you despite any regrets you may be having. If it's any consolation, we did use a condom last night after we had a late dinner."

Peaches turned to look at Tazz, feeling a sense of comfort that he didn't mean any harm. This was also a gentle side of him that she had never seen before. In fact, she never saw this side of any man before; not even the man she was so in love with, Drake. Tazz spoke softly and very respectfully when it came to her, and that was a plus considering the gorilla outfit he wore so well in the public eye.

All of the anger and feelings of betrayal started to fly right out the door the more Tazz comforted her with his kind words and charming grins in between jokes about what she had done last night when she was drunk. She, too, chuckled at the thought of singing to Tazz on the casino's floor with her heels off and clutched under her arm. It was funny because she couldn't sing to save her life, and although this was just one of the many stories Tazz had, she vaguely remembered it, along with a few other things she had done.

"What about your wife?" Peaches asked, remembering some of the conversation they had about her.

"Well, I didn't tell you everything, but she's supposed to be withdrawing more of my money today. I still don't understand why she has to steal from me when I give her whatever she asks me for. She has her own bank account that I put money into every month and she still wants more."

"So is that the reason why you're cheating on her with me, or is this something you do all the time?"

"You want me to be honest wit' you?"

"Yeah, I want you to be honest," Peaches demanded, not really sure if she wanted to hear the answer.

"Peaches, I would give up everything I own to be with someone like you. I've only known you for about a week, and by watching the way you carry yourself, I can see that you got ambition, you're smart, sexy as hell, and to be even more honest wit' you, the pussy got me open, and that was with a condom on! I never had a shot of pussy that had me waking up feigning. What you got them insides laced wit'? Crack?" Tazz said jokingly.

He pulled Peaches closer to him on the bed, admiring her naked body. All the talk about sex was making his dick hard, and although just minutes ago Peaches was upset, she didn't decline being wrapped up in his arms, if only for just that moment. If she had panties on at the time, Tazz would have talked them right off of her with no problem, given the fact she hadn't been treated like this in a long time. Peaches liked it, and for the moment she was going to make the best out of it.

Detective Codwell walked down 13th and Christian Street with a small notepad in his hand and a cigarette in his mouth, taking a good look around before being met by another detective who was first on the scene. "Tell me what you got," Codwell said, taking in a lungful of smoke.

"We got two dead bodies," the detective began as he pointed to the car. "Two males not identified yet. The driver was shot twice in his chest, and the passenger was shot in the back of his head."

"Did anybody see anything?" Codwell asked, looking into the car at the two dead bodies slumped over.

"This is where things get interesting. One lady said she saw a woman pull up in this car with the two dead guys in it. She got out and let the car roll down the street before jumping into some kind of SUV and pull off. The car rolled down the street and crashed into this parked car," he said, pointing with his finger as to how the incident took place.

"You're telling me that with all these people standing around, only one female saw what happened?"

"Well, from other interviews, nobody seemed to have heard any shots being fired. The car by itself has about twelve bullet holes in it, and there are no shell casings within a five block radius, so I don't believe the shootings took place here."

A call came over the detectives' radios asking for officers to respond to shots being fired on 23rd Street, which made the detectives look at each other and wonder if this had anything to do with the two dead bodies in front of them. Without further hesitation, they rushed to their cars and sped off.

Codwell's adrenaline was pumping the entire way to Tasker Avenue, with the anticipation of finding out who had committed a double murder in his part of the city. Whoever it was had the wrong detective on the case, because Codwell was known for getting his man.

Villain wasted no time speeding through the Lincoln Tunnel with nothing but murder on his mind and a .40 cal. on his lap. Blue Black, and anybody else that was in his surroundings, was in for more than they could handle.

The shipment of 200 bricks of cocaine was delivered to the club earlier that morning, and before he could even call Tazz to let him know the deal went down, Villain secured the coke and shot straight to New York. The cocaine deal was successful, and it was time to go to war.

He turned the radio down in the car when he heard his cell phone ringing. It was Tazz. Villain had been trying to contact him all day yesterday and this morning to remind him about the deal. "Damn, cannon! I been tryin' to get in touch wit' you all night," Villain said, answering the phone.

"Yo, I got caught up. What happened with the deal? Did Papi come through for us or what?"

"Yeah, I took care of everything and all of your kids are accounted for, safe, and in the house watching TV." Villain was speaking in code, basically letting Tazz know that the coke was secured.

Tazz was so caught up last night with Peaches that he had forgotten about the deal until this morning. Not only did her pussy take over his mind, it also made him forget about his money. "Where are you?" Tazz asked, hearing the sounds of car horns blowing in the background.

"I'm headed to Brooklyn right now," Villian said in a low voice, knowing that Tazz was going to have something to say about it.

"Yeah, I kind of figured that. You got somebody wit' you?"

"No, I'm rolling solo on this mission, big bruh. I'll see you in a few hours," he told Tazz, then hung up the phone.

Even though Villain knew that Blue Black was from Queens, he also knew about a couple spots in Brooklyn he hung out in, courtesy of Tazz's 411. The one thing about New York was that there were cops everywhere, and the hip-hop cops were just as bad.

Villain drove through Brooklyn in his rental car, a black Dodge Charger with tinted windows, hoping Blue would pop up at one of his strips to pick up money or drop off drugs.

He pulled into an apartment complex on Flatbush Avenue that Blue sold coke from; one of the many apartment buildings he ran throughout New York. At the entrance of the building was a young kid that looked like he was selling drugs, and when Villain got out of the car, low and behold, little man was making a sale. He did what anybody would do in his situation when Villain walked up to him. He reached for his gun, staring Villain up and down as though he was a stick-up kid.

"Whoa, whoa, youngin'! I ain't come here for that," Villain said, trying to ease the tension in the air, mainly because the young kid had the jump on him. "Look youngin', I'm tryin' to buy some weight. I just moved to the hood and I'm tryin' to get down," he said, knowing shorty couldn't cover the order and hoping that he would lead him straight to Blue.

"Dis Blue's neighborhood. You want parts of dis shit, you betta holla at him," shorty said, now pulling out a chrome .45 cal. "Nigga, I suggest you take ya bitch ass back where you came from before shit gets ugly out here."

Villain threw his hands up in the air, letting shorty know he was leaving. But the worst thing shorty could have done after pulling a gun out without using it was putting it back in his waistband and turning his back to Villain. He heard the shot, but didn't realize he was hit until he felt a burning sensation in his back, followed by the worst feeling of pain a man could feel. Shorty fell to the ground before he could reach for his gun.

Villain stood over him, clutching his hawk and pointing it directly at his face. "Tell Blue that da bull, Villain, came through here. You know what? Fuck it! Meet death!" Villain said, and fired a single shot into shorty's head.

The beef was on, and Villain was about to turn New York upside down until he found Blue. In the meantime, making every strip Blue owned hot with police was the plan until he showed his face. Anybody who was willing to ride out for Blue had better be ready to die for him as well, because Villain was ready to kill.

He left the murder weapon on shorty's chest and left the scene, but not before checking shorty's pockets and finding his cell phone. He left the money, drugs, and gun that shorty had on him. It was a sign for the homicide detectives, letting them know that it wasn't a robbery, but beef; something he did to taunt NYPD and to let Blue know it was on. And the fact that all this happened in broad daylight showed everybody how heartless, fearless, and gangster niggas on the streets could be.

Shorty's death was tragic, but he was a casualty of war. In fact, he was a soldier in war once he pulled his weapon in the name of Blue Black. It was ugly, but fair according to street rules.

Getting the money back to the United States was another problem in itself; because the most money one person can travel to the U.S. with was 10k, and anything more than that would draw a lot of attention, including the feds. One-point-five million wouldn't make it past the luggage check at the airport. The extra money it cost to get it back into the States was worth it, to a certain extent.

Patricia's people took 100k for changing the money over in Brazil, and then charged him an additional 400k for a guaranteed delivery into the U.S.

Drake's original cut was $2.5 million, but by the time the money went through Mexico and into Texas, 2 million was what he made out with. Veronica's $1.8 million was also reduced during this process, leaving her with a little over 1.3 million. Still, all in all the money didn't sound that bad for a few days worth of work.

Drake lay on the hotel room bed, counting the money they just picked up from Patricia's Mexican friend who brought the cash all the way to Dallas, Texas. The drive back to Philly would take a few days, which would bring the total amount of days working this job up to around a week. In order for that to have happened, Drake would need to be on the road in a couple of hours.

Veronica came out of the bathroom, drying off from a shower and baring more skin than the towel could cover. Drake did a double take as she crossed the room and stood in front of the mirror right behind him. Her breasts were slightly covered with the towel that was wrapped around her body, but he could see the curves that seemed to want to push through the towel. Her thighs were thick, and her ass was perfectly round, complimenting her small waist. Drake couldn't help but to admire her beauty. He turned around on the bed to watch Veronica blow-dry her wet hair.

She periodically caught him staring at her through the mirror. "Don't you think you're in enough trouble?" Veronica teased, unable to control the smile that came with it.

Drake didn't know what to say. His thoughts were being occupied by the hardening of his dick that he tried

75

so very hard to suppress. And Veronica standing right in front of him with nothing, but a towel wrapped around her was not making things any better. Losing his battle for self-control, he stood up and walked up behind her, and wrapped his hands around her waist.

Veronica turned the blow dryer around and playfully blew hot air in his direction. "Boy, you better stop before you get yourself in even more trouble. You know Kim's gonna kill you when you get back home."

"If she's going to kill me, then I better give her a reason to. She already thinks I'm sleeping wit' you."

Veronica turned away from the mirror to look Drake in his eyes. He was right because no matter what he could say to Kim, she wouldn't believe in a million years that we weren't sleeping together, she thought to herself, fighting the urge to steal a kiss. She wanted so badly to feel Drake's dick inside of her. "You don't want to do this," she said softly as she attempted to walk away, hoping that he really did.

Drake stopped her before she could go anywhere, wrapped his arms around her and pulled her body up against his. Her body went limp in his arms, as though she was beginning to melt.

The kiss that she wanted to steal was stolen, and the warmth of Drake's lips against hers made her pussy wet instantly.

Drake loosened the towel, letting it fall to the floor, exposing her breasts and pierced belly button. After gently pushing her onto the bed, he took his shirt off, then his pants, followed by his boxers, leaving Veronica's eyes focused on his large, thick dick that she wanted so badly. "Don't be scared," he said, climbing on top of her.

The thought of a condom crossed his mind for just a moment, until the head of his dick massaged the outside of her now dripping wet clit. He stuck half of his dick inside of her, making her moan lightly and almost giving her an orgasm before getting off a full stroke.

She grabbed onto his lower back and pulled his body closer, shoving the rest of his dick inside of her. Her moans turned into grunts as she tried to take it all in, but couldn't, even though her juices were flowing. As she tried to back up off of it, Drake chased her up the bed until there was nowhere else for her to go. With every stroke, the pain began to turn into pleasure. She wrapped her legs around his and dug her nails into his back while biting his shoulder and holding on for a ride that was going to be memorable.

Chapter 10

Tazz walked out onto the back porch where his wife was sitting at the table reading a book. This was the moment that he'd been waiting for. He was clutching the bank statements from today's withdrawal, showing $5 million dollars had been removed from their account as of yesterday morning. Although furious, he kept his cool, anticipating the excuse she was going to use for withdrawing so much money.

She lowered the book she was reading to see her handsome husband standing before her and she smiled, happy to see him because he hadn't come home last night. Her smile quickly turned into a frown when she saw the expression on his face filled with hurt. For a moment, Christina thought that someone in his family might have died, but then he passed her the bank statements without saying a word. It took her a few seconds to adjust to what he had given her, but she was confused at what she was reading. "What am I looking at, Tazz?" she asked, baffled.

"Tell me, Chris. Why do you need five million of our money? And furthermore, why do you have it in an offshore account?"

Christina looked at the paper, and then looked at Tazz, not believing what she just heard him say. She couldn't answer the question because she didn't know what to say.

But Tazz took it as a sign that she felt like she was caught. It wasn't the money that made him so angry, because five million was nothing compared to the money he had stacked up. He was angry because he felt betrayed by someone so close to him. He pulled a .38 revolver from out of his back pocket, placed it on the table and sat down in the chair right across from her. The one thing he hated more than a rat was a thief, and in his book when found, both of them should be shot.

"What's the gun for, Tazz? You think I'm stealing from you?" Christina asked, becoming angry at the thought. "After all these years, you got the nerve to think I would steal my own money? Oh, you must have forgotten that I put just as much work into our businesses as you did; and now you pull out a gun like you're gonna kill me if I did decide to spend any of our money? You know what? Fuck you, Tazz!" she said as she got up and headed into the house. "Oh, and for the record, no, Honey, I didn't take any money out of our account. I wouldn't dare do anything like that to the person I love enough to be his wife."

Tazz sat there with a dumb look on his face because everything she had said was true. It was she who helped

JOY DEJA KING AND CHRIS BOOKER

him build up the clubs from ground zero. She was there with him when he was still running around in the streets with nothing in his pockets. In reality, she was entitled to any and everything that he owned, not just because she helped him get to where he was, but more importantly, she was his wife. That's probably the only reason why he didn't shoot her.

He thought about everything she said and took into consideration that he didn't even question her about it in a respectful manner. What if she was telling the truth? What if she wasn't taking money from their account? How fair was it to just accuse her; and even worse, to threaten her life about it?

Just like he suspected, Detective Codwell found evidence at the 23rd Street shooting that linked to the two dead bodies on 13th Street. The only problem was the fact that nobody knew much of anything, except for the witness from 13th Street who could possibly identify the woman she saw getting out of the victims' car. The issue with that was they didn't know who they were looking for.

Codwell thought about Detective Grant. The woman he was looking for is from South Philly. She just might be the same woman he was looking for. The woman from the lounge shooting matched the same M.O. as the woman from the South Philly shooting, and that was basically a shoot to kill M.O.

Codwell drove around all day trying to get someone to talk, but the streets were on mute.

What Cindy did was knock the fight out of anybody else who wanted to step to her. Chris' boys, or the rest of his flunkies, now had more fear in their hearts than the need for revenge, and that's exactly how Cindy wanted it.

Codwell stood on the corner of 23rd Street with his cell phone to his ear, talking to Detective Grant and explaining what he was dealing with. Cop cars were still in the area and officers were still collecting evidence from the scene, when out of nowhere a white SUV went up Tasker Avenue, drawing Codwell's attention. It wasn't just the SUV that caught his eye, but the fact that it had what appeared to be bullet holes in it. He noted the license plate number. If it weren't for the fact that there was a lot of traffic going up Tasker Avenue and his car being parked on the other end of 13th Street, he would have surely chased down the SUV instead of merely putting an APB out for the car to all squad car radios.

Even so, things were looking up for him. A cop car parked in the vicinity heard the call over the radio. Seeing a truck that matched the description, he turned on his lights and got behind the truck.

Damn! Rick thought to himself as he looked into the rearview mirror at the cop car riding his tail. He was worried for a second because he realized that he still had a gun in the car, so he stepped on the gas.

Speeding through small city blocks at a high speed prompted the officer to back off of the truck slightly, but he still managed to give locations over the radio as to every street that the SUV turned down. "I'm in pursuit! I'm in pursuit of a white SUV heading west on Grays Ferry!" the officer yelled over the radio.

Hearing the call, almost every available car joined the chase, including Detective Codwell, who caught up with the chase in minutes.

Driving into the Southwest section of Philadelphia, Rick had about ten cop cars behind him like he was O. J. Simpson. His main objective was to get rid of the gun he had, so in order to do that, distance, swiftness, and total accuracy had to come into play when throwing the gun out of the window.

Being very familiar with the area, he turned down one street, then another, and then another, not losing the cop cars behind him but putting a little distance between them. This was his chance… his only chance.

The truck screeched onto a small street known for selling weed and crack, and just as he hoped, it was crowded with both drug dealers and addicts. Rick threw the gun from the driver's seat out through the passenger window that had already been shot out earlier. The gun landed under a parked car directly in front of several crackheads waiting to be served.

By the time the police turned onto the street, they were unaware of what Rick had done. The chase continued, and Rick drove the police as far away from the gun as he could. It was a no brainier that after the coast was clear of the cop cars racing down the street, one of the crackheads would grab the gun from under the car and eventually sell it moments later to one of the dealers.

The games were over. The cops wanted badly to end the chase before someone was seriously hurt, or even worse, ended up dead. The lead police car hit the rear of the truck, causing it to swerve out of control and smack into a parked car just one street over from another crowded street where children were playing.

The car chase was over, but that didn't stop Rick from trying to get out of the truck and run, but he was caught before he could get into stride.

Peaches looked down at her phone, unwilling to answer it because the number was blocked. It rang again, but this time a number showed up. "Hello," she answered, curious to know who was calling her with an out of state number.

"Yo, where you at?" Drake yelled into the phone, trying not to be drowned out by the sixteen-wheelers going up and down the highway.

"I'm at work right now."

"Work? Where the hell do you work at?" he asked, shocked more than anything.

Peaches had to think about what she had just said. She was, in reality, working for Tazz. "I'm working at the club… Tazz's club."

Drake forgot all about telling Peaches to keep a close eye on Tazz and to keep him busy if necessary while he sucked his bank account dry. Even still, the thought of her working for Tazz made him angry to the point where he really didn't want to talk anymore. If Drake only knew how she was keeping Tazz busy while he was gone, the shit would hit the fan.

"Alright, well quit ya job and take ya ass home. I'll be there in a couple of days," he said, then hung up in her ear.

She let out a sigh, looking at the empty club she just opened up this morning for regular business. Now, she was more confused than ever. She was actually starting to like her job.

Blue learned about one of his workers getting killed in the projects the other day, but it really meant nothing to him as he continued to blow money on any and everything. The twenty bricks of cocaine he had robbed from Villain were just about gone. He made a lot of money off of them, but his problem now was that he didn't have a connect to supply him with good coke. For a split second he almost regretted robbing Villain, seeing as though good coke was hard to come by.

Obtaining quality coke was the least of Blue's worries. It was just a week ago that he robbed a stone cold killer, and then had the nerve to kick him in the ass after doing so. It's one thing to rob a man, but to humiliate him in the process was even worse.

Blue pulled up to 133rd Street in Jamaica, Queens where most of his cocaine was being sold. He also grew up around this neighborhood, so it wasn't out of the ordinary when people gave him love every time he showed his face.

It just began to get dark, and Blue's workers were sitting in front of the apartment building taking turns serving customers. The silence that overtook the busy street grabbed Blue's attention almost instantly and everything started to move in slow motion. From both ends of the street, undercover narcotics police rushed down the block followed by regular patrol cars. The block was being raided.

Blue took off running thinking about the fact he was still on parole and he had a gun in his car. Everybody on the street scattered like roaches.

Blue sprinted through the apartment building, up to the second floor, down the hallway, and out of a window that put him on a fire, escape which lead him to the roof. It was an old getaway he used back when he sold drugs in front of the building. This route never failed, and today was no exception. He crossed over to the building next door, climbed through another window, went down the hallway, and knocked on apartment 5F's door. The door swung open. It was Shelly, a girl he fucked from time to time. But today wasn't a booty call.

Detective Codwell walked into the interrogation room where Rick was sitting.

Rick was holding an icepack on the side of his face and taking long drags of a Newport 100 that filled the room with smoke. He wasn't sure if they had found the gun he threw out of the window, so he just sat and listened instead of running his mouth.

"All I want to know is who's going to jail for a double homicide? You or Cindy?" the detective asked, taking a seat across from Rick.

That one question by itself sent chills down Rick's spine, but the one thing he didn't do was let the detective see that. It reminded him of a scene from the TV show, The First 48, but the only difference was that Rick did no talking whatsoever. He spoke only one word that everybody, even the detective in the next room watching and listening from a monitor, understood. "Lawyer!" he said, exhaling a cloud of smoke into the face of the detective.

"A lawyer won't help you, son. You've got to help yourself. The glass at the scene of the 23rd Street shooting matches the glass missing from the truck you were driving. The shell casings and bullet holes in your truck also match. The shell casings and bullet fragments that came from the two dead bodies on 13th Street match. I got a witness who can and will identify your little girlfriend and the truck leaving 13th Street. The guns found on the two dead bodies match the shell casings on 23rd Street. See, son, somebody is going down for those murders, and I know you had something to do with it," Codwell said, using every tactic in the book to get Rick to crack.

Rick took the icepack off of his face, put his cigarette out and looked the detective right in the eye. "If you know everything, why are you still sitting here talking to me? I'ma tell you one more time: I want to speak to a lawyer!" he demanded. He stood up from his chair, turned to the camera that was hoisted in the far corner of the room and said loudly, "Now!"

The one thing Detective Codwell didn't expect was for Rick to be so loyal, especially to a female. Most guys fold in the interrogation room when faced with doing double-digit numbers. But Rick possessed qualities only real street soldiers are bred with: loyalty, trust, honor and to protect your people at all cost. Codwell could see each one of these qualities in Rick, and for reasons outside of being a cop, he respected him for that.

The interview was over despite the fact that the lead detective in the precinct suggested that he go back in there and try to get a confession. Codwell knew from experience that Rick wasn't a talker. If he wanted to find out who Cindy was, he would have to be patient.

Chapter 11

There were about three people waiting to get a haircut in Blue's barbershop on 128th Street. This was the only legal business he had, and he wasn't that good at running it. The only thing he really did was come by on Fridays to pick up money from his barbers. Although it was rare, he did conduct a few drug deals in the back of the shop.

Business as usual, up until Villain walked through the front door, clutching a 9mm in one hand, a gallon of gasoline in the other, and a lit cigarette in his mouth. He quickly scanned the shop seeing that there were two barbers attending to customers, one woman and her young son sitting in the waiting chairs, and two guys watching TV in the back of the shop. There was a woman behind the register, and a large picture of Tupac hanging on the wall next to the bathroom.

"What can I do for you?" one of the barbers asked in a tone that displeased Villain.

Pow!

"Sit down!" Villain barked after shooting the barber in the leg.

One of the men in the back of the shop who had been watching TV, drew a .38 from his waist and aimed it in the direction of Villain. The only thing that stopped him from shooting was the woman and her son who were sitting right next to him by the front door. The guy was one of Blue's workers, and he was only there to get a quick haircut, but he got more than he bargained for.

Villain, on the other hand, didn't hesitate in squeezing several shots into the back of the shop, forcing the men to take cover.

He began pouring the gasoline all over the place, while at the same time keeping his eyes on the back of the shop and the guy with the gun who was lying behind a vending machine. He allowed everyone to leave the barbershop, except for the guys in the back. Then, he tossed his lit cigarette at the gasoline pooled on the barber station's countertop. The flames spread quickly throughout the shop, forcing Villain out the front door.

He sat across the street for a moment watching the shop burn. The two men who were left in it came running out through the flames and smoke. The sounds of sirens in the air grabbed his attention and reminded him that he was the one who set the fire, and the barbers amongst the crowd of onlookers—including the one he shot in the leg—would surely point him out to the cops. So, Villain faded out of the neighborhood like a ghost.

The one thing about Villain that people didn't know was that he was crazy, literally. Back in the old days, he was known for putting in big work out on the streets of Philly, and having most of the city scared when he came around. It was only a few years ago that he had changed. It wasn't the kind of change that made him become a good Christian, but the kind of change that made him become more business-minded, as opposed to killing any and everybody that stood in his way concerning the streets.

What Blue did was wake up an animal that would be hard to control once loose. If necessary, Villain was willing to burn all of New York to the ground in search of Blue, which in his eyes wouldn't be a problem at all. He knew of a few spots that Blue owned in the city; mostly drug houses or drug-infested corners where his product was being sold. Tazz also knew of a few spots that Blue had in the city, and that's how Villain knew about the barbershop. The beef was on, whether Blue liked it or not.

Tazz sat in the club looking over his bank statements, unable to track the money down after it left the Caymans. No trace at all. The money just vanished into thin air, which bothered him more than anything.

Christina hadn't really spoken to him ever since he blamed her for the money disappearing, but through it all, she didn't leave him nor slacked on her business responsibilities. Sexually, she was holding back and under the circumstances Tazz couldn't blame her. Being accused of stealing from your husband was a tough pill to swallow and only time would heal that wound.

Peaches walked into the club, disregarding Drake's instructions not to go back to work, but it wasn't work she was going back to. It was Tazz. Three days had passed since the night she and Tazz slept together, and in those three days he hadn't spoken to her nor called her in for work. It made her wonder what was going on. There was only one word to describe Peaches at this point, and that word was "open".

"You got what you wanted and now you act like you don't know me anymore?" she said, walking up and taking a seat next to Tazz in one of the V.I.P. booths.

The club was pretty much empty except for a few workers cleaning up for the weekend activities.

When she broke the silence in the room, it caught Tazz's attention. He was pondering so deeply on the bank statements that he didn't realize it was her until she sat down. It would be a lie to say that he wasn't happy to see her, because as soon as he laid eyes on her he smiled. He felt bitter about his money, but glad that she was there. "I'm sorry. I just been going through a lot," he said, setting his papers to the side. "I was going to call you into work this weekend. I need you to host some guests I got coming through on Saturday."

"Guests? Work? Is that all you want me for, Tazz? To host your little parties, look good for your guests and sleep with me when you feel like it?" she shot back.

"Whoa, whoa, Peaches! Am I getting attitude?" he asked jokingly, trying to ease the tension in the air. "Tell me what's going on, baby girl." He could see that she was starting to catch some type of feelings for him. He had only slept with her one time, and she was already feeling some type of way about him not acknowledging it, despite the fact that he was already married.

But Peaches was not alone in feeling the way she did. Tazz kind of felt the same, but didn't want to show it, mostly because he was still married. In all reality, he still loved his wife, whom he been with for several years.

"See, that's it right there, Tazz. You act all nice, treat me like you would treat a significant other, talk sweet to me, and you even gave me some of the best sex I ever had. And to top it off, you're a married man."

"So, what is it that you want from me, Peaches? I'm just as confused as you are. I like you a lot, and if I weren't married, I would probably try to wife you. You're beautiful, smart—"

"Yeah, yeah, you told me that already before," Peaches said, cutting him off. "I just want to know what happens now. Where do we go from here?"

Tazz put his head down and began to rub his temples. She was asking questions he didn't have the answers to right now. It didn't help much when his wife pulled up in front of the club, which he could see very well from the booth he was sitting in. She walked into the club toting a small plastic bag with food in it. Tazz had forgotten that they were supposed to have lunch today at the club, and talk about the situation with the missing funds from their account.

Christina walked up to the booth and laid his food out on the table, not even acknowledging the fact Peaches was sitting there.

Peaches acknowledged her though, speaking in a soft voice. Christina spoke back and gave a smile. The one thing about Tazz's wife was that she was never insecure about her husband's interactions with other women, seeing as though he was in the entertainment business. She knew he would come into contact with plenty of beautiful girls, but she refused to be the type of wife that tracked his every move. She had one simple rule, if he ever got caught cheating, she would leave and be done with him the very first time so it could never happen a second time.

Plus, Christina was gorgeous in her own right, and frankly, prettier than 99% of women that Tazz came into contact with, and she knew it. Tazz knew it, and now Peaches knew it too. Based on her appearance alone, Peaches could see why Tazz had married her.

"Well, I'ma let you have lunch. What time do you want me to come in on Saturday?" Peaches asked, using her best exit strategy.

"I'm thinking around 8:00, but I'm not sure. I'll give you a call tomorrow and let you know for sure what's goin' on."

She got up and left, feeling sad more than anything. Here I go again, falling for a man who's already taken, she thought to herself as she walked out the front door. She was tired of coming in second place when it came to relationships. In her heart, she felt like she deserved to be number one, but what she couldn't understand was why she allowed herself to accept being the number two girl. Being second to Kim for so long, while dealing with

Drake made her forget about her capabilities of being able to satisfy a man enough so that he wouldn't want to be with more than one woman; and with Drake being out of town for the past week, it gave her the chance to enjoy the experience of dropping her guard and letting her mind run free in the company of another man.

There was no question that Peaches loved Drake with all of her heart. It was just time for her to fight for the things she desired to have in a relationship, which was to be the "only" one instead of being number one, and definitely not number two. Hell, Peaches looked just as good, if not better, than both Christina and Kim, but deep down Peaches knew it took much more than beauty to keep a man. Playing second fiddle for so long had broken her self-esteem. Being able to get a man wasn't going to be a problem, but finding the right one was the challenge.

Cindy stayed at her cousin Hassan's house in South Philly after seeing Rick on the news getting chased by the cops. The last thing that would pop in her mind was whether or not Rick would tell on her about the shooting. He had always proven to be loyal, but sometimes even the best of men fold under the right amount of pressure.

Hassan was Cindy's first cousin, and they were the same age, but stayed in different parts of South Philly. He was more of a rapper than anything, but outside the booth, he lived every bit of the life he proclaimed he lived in his songs. Gunplay was his M.O., and although he dressed like a bum in the streets, his money was longer than most of the niggas in Philly.

It wasn't even a month ago that Hassan walked out of the Criminal Justice Center after winning a jury trial for a double homicide back in 2008.

Not too long ago, he found Allah and the Messenger Muhammad while he was in jail. But a lot of guys do that. They come home and roll with Shaytaan. Hassan was on his dean for the most part, but from time to time he'd fall back into his old ways, shaking down drug dealers he knew from back in the day and applying his own personal street taxes. Dudes would rather pay the taxes once in a while rather than have Hassan back in the streets full time. It would be hard trying to make a dollar with him running around all day and night, sticking guns in people's faces and his hands in their pockets.

Cindy's phone rang. The number was blocked which made her not want to answer it, but she knew Rick would be calling any time now with a bail. She already had Fredrick Perry and Brian McMonigal on standby. They were the top lawyers in the city, specializing in homicides, drugs, and robbery cases. They had both been on Cindy's payroll for years now, and this would be the first time she had to use them.

"Who's this?" she answered, sitting on the couch watching the television.

"My bail is $150,000," Rick said into the phone, and then hung up before she could ask any questions. He knew that the homicide detectives were recording any conversation he had, seeing as though they didn't have enough evidence to charge him with the murders. What they did charge him with was eluding the police and resisting arrest. When asked in the interrogation about the double homicide, he didn't say anything, and that was the key to him not being charged with the murders just yet.

"Yo, I need you to go downtown and pay Rick's bail for me," she told Hassan who just walked into the room.

"How much is his bail?"

"One-hundred fifty-thousand, but ten percent of that is 15,000."

"You want me to take you to get the money, or do you need a loan for a couple of days?" Hassan asked before laughing.

Cindy grabbed her purse, reached inside and pulled out a wad of money. Fifteen thousand was nothing to her. She usually had that much on her at any given time; merely just play money for the most part. She had to act fast to bail Rick out, because the longer he sat in the police station, the longer the detectives had access to him if they wanted to question or maybe even give him more charges.

"Look, lil' cousin, when Rick gets out, I got some work that needs to be put in that could be beneficial for you," she said, counting out 15,000. "I know you're doing your Muslim thing and tryin' to do right by God, but I also know the hood fears you, and you still get ya hands dirty every now and again."

Hassan smiled. "You don't know nothing, cousin," he smiled.

"I know that your dad and my mother come from the same womb, which means that the same blood that flows through your veins is the same blood flowing through mine. I'm about to take over the whole city, and I want you to ride out wit' me. We can split the city up 50/50."

"Cuz, I'm not tryin' to be rude, but I'm Muslim, and 50% of the city is what I don't need," Hassan said, no longer joking and taking a seat on the couch next to her. "I got money, I got power, and I got respect. I do what I do in the streets sometimes, but I could never make the streets my wife again. I just fuck it when I want to, then keep it moving. You got to understand that these streets don't last forever. One day you're going to have to meet Allah, and on that day you won't be able to ransom none of what you got from these streets for a spot in Paradise…"

Here he goes wit' the bullshit! Cindy thought to herself. Although everything Hassan was saying was the truth, at this point, all Cindy could think about was getting Rick out of jail and paying a visit to a few old friends.

"Cuz. Cuz!" Hassan said, snapping his fingers and bringing Cindy out of the daze she fell into while he was talking. "Look, I love you, even though you don't come around that much," he said, now smiling again. "If you need me, I'm here for you. Whatever you need; just let me know. But know that I'm here for you because we are family, and not for any other reason."

Chapter 12

Drake and Veronica came through the Pennsylvania Turn¬pike feeling relieved to be back home. The journey was long and hard, and neither one of them wanted nothing more than to curl up in their own beds and get some good sleep.

The first person Drake tried to call was Kim. Ever since she found out that he was with Veronica, she hadn't answered her cell phone or the house phone. He was more worried about her and the baby's wellbeing than anything else . He then tried to call Peaches, she being the next person he wanted to check up on. The phone rang a few times then went to her voicemail.

"What's wrong?" Veronica asked, seeing the angry look on his face when he tossed the phone onto the dashboard.

It was more than just the cross-country trip back to the city that gave him a headache. It was the stress of knowing that Kim was mad at him to the point of not wanting to talk to him, and the fact that Peaches was missing in action. The first thing he wanted to do was put up the money he had in the trunk, get Veronica home, and get a couple hours of sleep before dealing with his women problems.

"Everything's good. I'ma put this money up and get you home. I got a lot of shit to take care of, so what I want you to do is refrain from going on ya shopping spree for a couple of days. Act normal so you won't draw any attention on yourself," Drake told her, being cautious.

Veronica just stared at him while he drove. They both had fought the temptations of fucking again. During the entire trip back home, they stayed in separate hotel rooms per Drake's request, and that was something Veronica didn't understand, seeing as their sexual chemistry was incredible. She was hoping for more. She wanted Drake to feel the same way she felt, but she also realized that he loved Kim, and they were about to be a family once she had his baby, which was a bitter sweet moment. The silence in the car took over. Veronica wanted so badly to tell him what was going on in her mind, but she refused to be a home wrecker, even though she may have already done so by sleeping with Drake.

"Look, Drake. We can't just act like nothing ever happened between us," she said, breaking the silence. "But what we can do is try to maintain a friendship, as opposed to letting regret break us apart. I always want to be your friend, even if that's all we can be. Oh, and by the way, I'll talk to Kim and let her know that nothing happened between us," she told him while looking out of the window. "Give this to her," she said, reaching into her pocketbook and passing Drake a jewelry box with one of the diamond bracelets she had bought from Tiffany's the first time she took money out of Tazz's account. "Diamonds are a girl's best friend, and a cure for a broken heart. Trust me."

Villain was still wearing the same clothes he had on for the past few days, along with the same funk that came from not taking a shower within those days. He pulled up to the apartment buildings on 133rd Street in Jamaica, Queens, hoping that Blue was going to be out there.

There was a lot of traffic going up and down the street, mainly crackheads coming to score from the several dealers sitting in front of the building. There was so much traffic that no one even noticed Villain sitting on the corner of the block. He didn't jump right out of the car, but rather waited and watched the movements of the dealers.

Every so often one of them would walk off and grab some drugs out of the trunk of a car parked just a couple of cars in front of Villain. The security was mild, with a shooter on the balcony of one of the apartments, another lookout on the ground in front of the building, and the possibility of the dealers being strapped. The nighttime darkness helped Villain's car blend in with rest of the cars on the block.

Villain got out of his car, opened up the trunk and grabbed an M-90, cocking a bullet into the chamber. He closed the trunk and stood at the side of his car and waited. He knew that he didn't have long to make his move with all the crackheads passing by him on their way to the apartments. One of them would surely tell a dealer that I'm down here with a large gun, he thought to himself.

He walked down the sidewalk on the opposite side of the block. As soon as he got directly across the street from the apartment building, he opened fire into the crowd. Before the shooter on the balcony could see where the shots were coming from, Villain sent a couple of shots in his direction, forcing him to take cover inside the apartment.

As expected, two of the three drug dealers had guns and wasted no time firing back at Villain. The bullets flew by his head just missing him, but the guns they had were handguns; nothing that could compete with the assault rifle Villain had, which carried one hundred shots.

Villain stood in the middle of the street, going head up and knocking holes in the concrete building and shattering a few windows.

After the dealers fired all of their shots, they took off running in different directions. Villain also took off, but not running. He walked calmly back to his car, gun in hand like he had a license to shoot at drug dealers. Tossing the gun into the trunk, he took a cigarette out of his pocket and lit it, taking long drags and leaning up against the car, not afraid of anybody or anything. He waited until he heard police sirens getting closer to get into his car and pull off before they swarmed the block.

Drake walked into the house hoping to be greeted by Kim, but his hope fell short after checking the entire house and seeing that she wasn't there. His blood began to boil, and a shot of fear ran through his heart, thinking something might have happened to her.

He sat on the bed and noticed a note with a phone number on the nightstand. "I'm in the hospital," it read.

He quickly picked up the phone and dialed the number, relieved to hear Kim's voice answer the phone. "What's going on? Why are you in the hospital? Is the baby here? Is something wrong? Why aren't you answering your cell phone?" he asked, not giving her time to answer one question before asking another.

"Drake, calm down. I'm alright. The baby is fine. I just had a false alarm. The doctors are going to run a few tests and I'll be home shortly. My sister is here and she's going to bring me home."

"I'm coming to get you right now," Drake insisted.

"Don't come up here, Drake, and don't act like you care about what's going on with me when you're vacationing with your little girlfriend. If I meant anything to you, you would have been here instead of out cheating," Kim argued, still mad at him. "And don't insult my intelligence and tell me you didn't sleep with that girl, because I know you did."

"Baby, just come home so we can talk," Drake pleaded, trying not to make her anymore upset than what she already was.

Kim thought about it for a split second. "No, Drake. I'm not coming home tonight. I really don't feel like being bothered by you right now. Go talk to Veronica," she said, and then hung up the phone.

Drake felt like shit. He didn't realize how badly he messed up, and he surely didn't realize how much of an effect Kim had on him up until now. Just the thought of losing her brought tears to his eyes. He wanted for them to be a family. And although Kim didn't know it, Drake planned on leaving the streets alone after she had the baby. He was even prepared to let Peaches go and actually try his best to be faithful.

He just sat on the bed and stared at the blank TV screen until his cell phone rang. It was Veronica. He really didn't want to answer the phone. He didn't feel like talking to anybody right now, but he had to. He had to stop Veronica from trying to contact Kim to tell her that they didn't sleep together. Kim wasn't stupid by far, and telling her a lie when she feels differently would be a sign of disrespect in her eyes.

"Hello," Drake answered, not in a good mood.

"Are you home?"

"Yeah, Veronica, I'm home. Look, don't call Kim. She's not tryin' to hear anything you or I have to say. Let me take care of it. I fucked up, so I think I should be the one to fix it. "

"I can respect that. I was just calling to let you know that I'm moving out of the city in a couple of weeks. It's nothing you did. I had plans on doing this for a while now. Now that I have the money, I think now would be the best time."

Drake and Veronica shared a different type of bond than what he had with other women, mainly because it didn't involve sex… at least up until a few days ago. They possessed similar qualities outside of a sexual attraction. It was a friendship, just two people that shared the same concepts on life. The news shocked him, but he had no other choice but to accept it, seeing as there was nothing he could do about it. He already had enough problems with Kim and Peaches right now, so the best thing to do was to let her go, despite his personal feelings about the situation.

When Hassan got down to the Criminal Justice Center to pay Rick's bail, he found out that Rick had a detainer for a charge he caught in New Jersey a few years back. Even if his bail were paid, they wouldn't let him out until he went to New Jersey to deal with that charge. This put a small dent into Cindy's plans for taking over the city, but it wouldn't stop her from pushing forward.

Chapter 13

Cindy pulled up in front of the pizza joint in an all black Beamer, solo, but strapped with a chrome .45. Her intention wasn't violence, but rather to discuss business with Max.

South Philly has been treating her well, and seeing as it was time to expand, that only meant it was time to step her game up and get a better connect that could supply the large amount of cocaine she needed. Max couldn't do it. For the most part, Max was only buying between fifty and one hundred bricks of cocaine every couple of months, and if she wanted to, Cindy could buy that much every month, guaranteed. Her only problem was getting Max to share the wealth and give up his connect. Doing so would probably end up putting him out of business because when Cindy said she was going to take over the entire city, that's exactly what she meant. North Philly, South Philly, West Philly, Southwest Philly, Germantown, Northeast Philly, Logan, West Oaklane, and even downtown Center City were all the spots she had her

JOY DEJA KING AND CHRIS BOOKER

eyes on, and in some cases she already had her hands in a few of those sections.

The sounds of steaks being chopped up on the grill, pizza ovens being opened, and cash registers ringing filled the air when Cindy walked through the door. To the eyes of someone who didn't know any better, they would have thought this was an official business, and besides all the cocaine being pumped out of the back door, the food was pretty good. To get what you want, you just had to know the right thing to say. Max's cocaine business was based on coded slang, and the only way you could come into Max's world was if you knew someone who knew someone, and that person knows Max; or if you spoke the right words and those words always came from Max himself.

In Cindy's hand was a pizza box that came from his store. "I asked for a ground beef pizza and these are pepperonis," she said, laying the box on the counter. "Is it possible that I can speak to a manager?"

"Ma'am, we can change the order for you if you like," the cashier said, taking a look inside the box.

"Look, I don't want my order changed. I just want to speak to the manager."

This conversation seemed normal to the average customers that were waiting for their food. But the same conversation meant something more serious. Being sold a pepperoni pizza instead of ground beef really meant that she didn't like the product, and something was possibly wrong with it. Asking for the manager meant that she wanted to speak with Max. When the cashier offered to change the order that meant he would replace the coke, but Cindy refused and continued to ask for the manager, which meant there was a serious problem.

She was lead to the back of the pizza shop where Max's office was located. Standing outside of the office door was an armed bodyguard that patted Cindy down before she could enter. He removed a .45 automatic from off her hip.

Max was sitting at his desk doing some typing on the computer when she walked in. He heard the entire conversation she had with the cashier, thanks to the audio and video surveillance system he had installed throughout the shop, which he could monitor right from his desk. It was a shock to see that Cindy had a complaint, since he'd always done good business, and had so with Cindy for the past couple of years... at least that's how Max felt.

"Take a seat. What can I do for you, young lady?" Max said, taking his eyes off of the computer screen and focusing them on Cindy.

"Look, Max. I been doing business with you for a while now, and I always came straight. My money was right every time I copped from you."

"Get to the point, kid. What do you want from me?" he asked, being very short.

"I want you to introduce me to your connect. I need somebody who can supply me with what I need."

"You know I can't give you my connect. I own South Philly. Anything you need, I'll supply you," he said, starting to become irritated with what she was asking.

Cindy, too, was starting to get irritated at the way Max was talking to her and becoming a little aggressive in his tone of voice. Although she expected him to turn her down, it still was a tough pill to swallow hearing him say that he owned South Philly. Max barely even steps foot out of the pizza shop to even know what's going on in the streets, and he damn sure ain't put no work in lately, she thought to herself, listening to Max go on and on about how much of a boss he was.

"You know what, Max? You're right. I don't know why I came down here thinking you would help somebody who might be getting more money than you," she said, and stood up to leave. "I probably would do the same thing if I was you. But for the record, and I need you to hear me when I say this: I run South Philly. And if you think selling coke out of a pizza shop gives you the right to own South Philly, think again." She raised her shirt to show the bullet wound from the Broad Street shootout. "Only blood, sweat, and tears can give you the right to say that you own anything, and I've done all three." She then walked out of the office and grabbed her gun from the guard on her way out.

What Max didn't understand was that Cindy was on a mission. Max couldn't see past his little drug operation to know that South Philly was being dominated by a young black woman who wasn't afraid to pop her pistol. He also didn't catch on that this visit from Cindy today was his only opportunity to keep his business alive once she gained control over the city. He had better chances of giving up his connect than he did staying alive.

Drake walked up the five flights of stairs to get to Peaches' apartment. He did kind of miss her and was hoping she was there. Most of the time he just used his key, but tonight he decided not to, thinking that he would surprise her when she opened the door.

The sound of music playing came from the apartment, so he knew that she was home. He knocked, but nobody answered. He knocked a few more times before getting fed up, so he whipped his key out, stuck it in the door, unlocked it and walked in.

The living room was dark, but the light from the bathroom helped to show him where the light switch on the wall was, which he turned on.

He walked over to the stereo system and turned the music down, expecting Peaches to come out of the bedroom any minute, but she didn't. Something was wrong, he thought to himself, pulling a black 9mm from his waist. Turning the music all the way off, he could finally hear what was going on in the bedroom.

"Oh, Daddy! Oh, Daddy!" Peaches yelled out, sending a sharp pain through Drake's chest. "Dis is ya pussy, Daddy! Dis is all ya pussy!" she continued.

For a moment Drake didn't know what to do. Her voice echoing through the apartment sent chills up his spine, and the first thing that came to his mind was to kill her and whoever else was in there. He looked around and grabbed a pillow from off of the couch so that he could muffle the sound of the gunshots. The closer he got to the door, the louder Peaches screamed, making Drake even madder. This was it, the moment of truth.

He grabbed the knob of the bedroom door and turned it. His palms were sweaty, his legs felt like wet noodles, and for a brief moment his heart stopped beating, at least that's how it felt. No more games.

He flung the door open. He raised his gun, already cocked and ready to shoot. What he saw was too much for him to handle. What he saw made him snap...

"I got her! I got her!" Detective Codwell loudly announced as he ran into the office where his partner was sitting. "Cynthia McParson. Rick called her cell phone yesterday. Her last known address is in Mt. Airy," he said, throwing a photocopy of her driver's license on the desk.

"So we bring her in and see if our witness can identify her as the woman leaving the scene in the white truck," his partner added, grabbing his jacket off the back of his chair. "If we can I.D. her, then we surely got a case."

Detectives Grant and Hill went back to the hospital, only to find the man from the Broad Street shooting had died. He died late last night, and the doctor said that his last words were, "Girl... girl," which were the same words he managed to get out during their last visit.

Grant was leaving the hospital when his cell phone started ringing. Just when he thought he was at a dead end, it was Codwell on the phone. He told Grant all about the South Philly shooting, and how they might have a suspect, and a woman who could possibly identify Cindy. He told him about how Cindy's M.O. of a heartless killing was similar to the woman he was looking for. Grant was even more determined to get a hold of this suspect so he could interrogate her about the murders.

It was very common for detectives all over the city to work with and help one another, especially when it came to homicides. Sometimes a detective would turn his head if another one were doing something outside of protocol. That's just the way police worked in the city of Philadelphia.

Tazz's dick went limp mid-stroke at the sight of Drake standing in the doorway with a gun pointed directly at him. This was the part where he regretted cheating on his wife.

Peaches lay beneath him with a dumb expression on her face. Before she could say a word, Drake advised her not to, and she willingly obliged knowing that if she did so, it would probably cost her life if Drake decided to let her live. Tazz didn't know what to do, but he was smart and followed the same instructions that Drake gave Peaches.

Drake walked over to the nightstand next to the bed and grabbed Tazz's gun, along with his wallet and car keys. Drake then took a seat in a chair next to the bed, holding the two guns in his hands. He wanted to take a minute and get himself together by taking in all that was in front of him.

His girl was lying naked with a man that he just took five million from, and had plans on robbing him for a large amount of cocaine. They were having sex in the apartment that he pays the rent for. They were also having sex in the bed that he also paid for, along with the rest of the bedroom set. She had the nerve to have a picture of Drake as big as day on the dresser. And most of all, she was having unprotected sex, and was sleeping with the enemy. All those factors rushed through Drake's head at once, giving him a slight headache.

Everything that Peaches ever said about love, loyalty, honor, trust and faithfulness went right out the door, and by the way he was looking at her, she could see exactly the way he felt. Tears began to pour down her face, and the feeling of being disloyal to a man she felt was like a husband took over. She wanted to die. She wanted Drake to end this feeling by pulling the trigger.

But Drake had other plans. "Get dressed," he said, pointing the gun in the directions of where their clothes were lying across the room.

When Tazz got up and walked over to grab his clothes off of the floor, it was the first time that he noticed the picture of Drake on the dresser. He also noticed the calm aura Drake displayed for a man who just caught his girl cheating. It was the kind of calm Tazz knew nothing good would come out of.

After they both got dressed, Drake made them both sit down on the bed in front of him like they were two kids about to be punished by their mother.

The thug in Tazz could only hide for so long. He was far from being a pussy. In fact, the memory of one of his old girlfriends in the same situation came to mind. The outcome wasn't good. "So now what?" he asked, breaking the silence in the room, lifting his head up to look Drake in the eyes.

"I don't know, big guy. You tell me since you're the one layin' wit' ya dick all up in my chick."

"I'm only here 'cause she wanted me here," Tazz said, looking at Peaches with angry eyes.

"Check dis out, big guy. Since you got a lot to say, tell me how much ya life means to you. I'm not a playa hater. You fucked my chick and I congratulate you. But know for sure that since I caught you, it's going to cost you. It may cost you a lot, or it may cost you a little, but it's definitely gonna cost you," Drake said with a smile on his face. "I'm sure you from the streets. Peaches here don't mess wit' soft-core niggas. Do you, Peaches?" he asked while pointing the gun at her.

"So, what are you sayin' dog?" Tazz asked him.

"What I'm sayin' is that seeing as you from the streets, you should already know the game. Make me an offer for your life, or get ya head blown off right here, right now. It's that simple."

"Man, I don't have nothing," Tazz said, not knowing that Drake knew almost everything about him.

Drake stood up, took the safety off of the gun and pointed it right at the center of his forehead. Peaches turned her head to avoid watching Tazz get shot. She knew that Drake always means what he says.

"Wait!" Tazz yelled out, hoping that Drake wouldn't pull the trigger. "Just tell me what you want." He could see the anger in Drake's eyes even though his face was totally relaxed.

Although Tazz was gangsta in his own right, he still wasn't prepared to die, especially over a chick he didn't even know that well. He was willing to give up everything he had in order to walk out of the door in one piece, and that's exactly what he offered... or at least half of it for starters. "Do you sell drugs? Do you want drugs? I got some drugs," he stuttered, as his thoughts were too fast for his mouth to utter.

"How much drugs?" Drake asked, pressing the barrel of the gun up against his forehead.

"I'll give you one hundred bricks of pure cocaine. Just let me go."

Drake smiled, knowing that Tazz had more than one hundred bricks, according to what Peaches told him; unless he sold one hundred bricks in a few days, which was highly unlikely. So in reality he had to have two hundred bricks of cocaine, give or take a few. Nevertheless, Drake wanted it all, and Tazz wasn't going to leave the room alive until he had it.

Silence fell over the room once again. Drake was thinking of a way to strip Tazz of everything he had. He sat back down in the chair in front of the bed, scratching his head with the gun and pondering on what to do next.

Peaches continued to sit there without saying a word. For a moment he looked over at her to see tears still falling down her face. She was too ashamed to even look at him. When she finally glanced over at him, the eye contact said a thousand words, and with a wink of his right eye at her, she instantly became relieved. That wink was confirmation that she was going to live.

Chapter 14

Villain finally decided to check into a hotel room for a shower, a good dick suck, and a couple hours of sleep before he got back out on the streets in search of his now worst enemy, Blue.

He called Little Mike at the club just to check up on things since Tazz wasn't answering his phone. He figured that he was probably out with Christine doing some shopping or something.

When Little Mike answered the phone, he sounded worried. "Yo, Villain, where is everybody?" he asked. "There's nobody at the club. I haven't seen Tazz since last night. He wasn't even here this morning to open up. I had to call Christina, and she did it."

"Don't worry about it. I'll be back in the city in a few hours," Villain said while guiding the back of a chick's head up and down on his dick.

"Yo, Villain man, I think something's wrong. It just don't feel right. I been tryin' to call Tazz all morning and he hasn't answered not one time."

"Didn't I just say I'll be there in a few hours?" Villain shouted, and then hung up the phone.

The dick suck was feeling a lot better than what Mike was talking about. He just lay there and observed Missy's bobbing technique, and couldn't help feeling her warm throat and juicy lips suffocating his dick, forcing him to bust a nut clear down her throat.

Missy was a pro at sucking dick, and every time Villain was in New York he would call her, knowing she would get him right. That's all she was really good for anyway, seeing as she was the neighborhood hood rat who would fuck for a buck, and would also do some strange things for that change. Not too many niggas fucked her, although she had a fat ass and some big titties. Her main art was dick sucking, and that's exactly what she was going to do for the next couple of hours... or at least until Villain fell asleep.

Villain still couldn't help but to think about what Mike said. It wasn't that strange for Tazz to be missing in action all night, but it was out of character for him to not be there to open the club up, which was something he hardly ever missed doing first thing in the morning. All this would have to wait to be dealt with later. First thing's first: a couple of hours of sleep.

Nothing seemed right when Cindy woke up in the morning. She was used to waking up alone in her humongous four-bedroom house in the more conservative part of Mt. Airy, so the eerie feeling wasn't coming from that. It felt like a storm of darkness had knocked on her front door, but she didn't want to let it in. Cindy began to reason that maybe it was a warning that danger was looming.

Trying to fight off the negative vibe, just like every day, Cindy got out of bed, took a shower, dressed, and grabbed a bite to eat while reading the newspaper that was delivered this morning to her front door.

The feeling of someone watching her made her very uncomfortable. So she went back upstairs to retrieve one of the many guns she kept in a walk-in closet. The .45 ACP was her gun of choice when lying around the house. Placing it in her back pocket, she looked out of every window downstairs in hopes of finding what was making her so uneasy.

Today, Rick had a court hearing to determine whether or not he could be released on house arrest while awaiting trial. First, he would have to see the judge for the violation charges he caught for the current case before he could pay the bail on the new case and get released. He violated his probation, so the chances of him getting released were slim, but worth the try. Cindy surely was going to be there to see the outcome of it.

She walked outside to get into her car, and before she could lift the driver's side door handle to get in; she looked around and spotted a white man standing at the edge of her driveway, smoking a cigarette.

Seconds later, police came from everywhere with their guns drawn and pointed directly at her. They came from the sides of her house, from behind cars parked on the street, and from out of the neighbors' backyards. They were swarming like she was on the ten most wanted-list.

Surprisingly, Cindy was relieved that it was only the police and not some thugs from the streets coming to rob her, or even kill her for that matter. She almost made a crucial mistake by reaching in her back pocket and grabbing the .45 ACP she still had on her.

"Get your fucking hands in the air or I'll blow your fucking head off!" one officer yelled. He was not taking any chances with Cindy, knowing the possibility of her having killed several people in the past few weeks. Neither he nor the other cops were willing to take that risk.

Detective Codwell, who was standing at the end of her driveway, noticed the bulge in her back pocket and could actually see a part of the handle of the gun. "Don't do something you might regret," he said as he slowly approached Cindy.

The one thing about Cindy was that she was far from stupid. She complied with every instruction given to her by the officers, from putting her hands on the top of her head to getting down on her knees. She watched too many people get shot by police on YouTube, all because they didn't comply fast enough.

Once inside the back of Codwell's car, she immediately asked for an attorney before he could ask the first question.

"Why would you ask for a lawyer when you're not even under arrest yet?" Codwell asked, looking in his rearview mirror at Cindy sitting next to one of the police officers who arrested her.

"If I'm not under arrest, why am I sitting in the back of this police car with handcuffs on?"

"This is just procedure for questioning someone who had a gun on them. Tell me, Cindy, do you have a license to carry?" he asked, thinking she would say no.

"Yeah, I got a license to carry, and the gun you took from me is registered in my name. And what do you mean by 'procedure for questioning'? What do you wanna question me about?"

"You'll find out when we get to the station."

The rest of the ride back to the police station was quiet. Cindy had already had a feeling what she was going to be questioned about, but she also knew her rights.

In the meantime, during the ride to the station the officer took down all of Cindy's information and had already begun writing his arrest report, thinking that she was surely going to be charged.

Word got out at the police station that they had Cindy in custody, so when they pulled into the parking lot, there were officers lined up to see what she looked like. Even though she was only being brought in for questioning, it was totally up to her whether or not she would leave.

After checking to see if she was licensed to carry a weapon and if the gun was registered in her name, Detective Codwell walked into the interrogation room with a smile on his face, and a lit cigarette in his mouth. He conducted many interrogations before with women, but none of them were anything like Cindy.

She sat in the room with her nipples rock-hard from the cold air blowing out of the vent. She didn't even consider drinking the cup of water provided, nor did she smoke any of the cigarettes lying on the table. She just sat there and didn't say a word.

"You know why you're here don't you, Cindy?" Codwell began. "You've been very busy as of late. Well, I'm going to get straight to the point. Rick already told us about the shootout on 23rd Street, and how you were the one who shot those two guys and dumped their bodies on 13th Street. I also got a witness from the scene who saw you getting into Rick's SUV after dumping the bodies. Look, I'm not saying that you did it, but all the evidence is pointing towards you. If you give me your side of the story, maybe we can help you out."

It was really a bunch of word play that Cindy was all too familiar with. She wasn't falling for any of it. She just sat there without saying a word. She was well aware of the street code of not talking to the police, and she knew that Rick would never tell on her, like detective Codwell wanted her to believe.

Cindy's silence made him even more upset. "You know, we're checking the ballistics on that .45 we took from you today. That's the same type of gun used in the murders!" he yelled, smacking the cup of water off of the table in an effort to try and scare her.

Cindy just sat there and didn't say a word.

At that point, Detective Grant walked into the room, taking off his jacket, placing it on the back of the chair and taking a seat right in front of Cindy. He threw a stack of photos onto the table.

A picture of Chris lying on the floor with a gunshot wound to the neck caught Cindy's attention when it slid in front of her. She looked at the pictures, smiled, and then pushed them back across the table. "I guess this is the part where I'm supposed to confess to you that I did it," she said, still smiling. "You guys are so fucking weak. I ain't confessing to shit."

"If you are done questioning my client, which I'm sure you are now that I'm here, I believe we are ready to leave if she's not under arrest," McMonigle said after entering the interrogation room and showing his identification.

"Your client is at the center of a murder investigation—"

"Yeah, yeah, and as I said before, if you're not charging my client, she should be free to go," McMonigal interjected.

The two detectives huddled for a moment, coming to the conclusion that they didn't have any evidence on Cindy except for the crackhead who said she saw a female getting into a white truck. They were allowed to keep her in custody for 48 hours so that they could find the crackhead and do a line-up, and that's exactly what they did. The chances of them finding their witness would be slim to none, but it was all they could do for now. It was either that, or to watch Cindy walk right out the door.

It was late morning, and Villain was on his way back to Philly to see what was going on with Tazz, who was still unreachable. After that, Villain was definitely going right back to New York to continue his mission on finding

Blue and flat out kill him. He didn't want the cocaine back. He didn't want the money or the possibility of interest. All he wanted was for Blue to look down the barrel of his gun and plead for his life before getting his whole face blown off.

Villain was a mere five blocks away from getting onto the Brooklyn Bridge when he noticed a cop pulling a car over. He was cautious of these types of things when he was riding dirty. He thought to himself how nice the car getting pulled over was, and as he rode by the S.550 Benz, he swore his eyes were playing tricks on him when he saw Blue in the driver's seat. He quickly went around the block in order to get another look before he did one of two things, which was either continue heading home, or kill Blue right there right then.

Coming up on the Benz again, he looked inside and there he was. It was Blue. Villain's heart started to race. His adrenaline started pumping through his body and the taste of victory was on the tip of his tongue.

He pulled his car over onto a side street just one block away, got out and popped the trunk. Inside was the M-16 now fully reloaded, two twin .40 cals., and a bulletproof vest that he quickly put on. He looked around before pulling out the M-16, and when he saw no one, he slammed the trunk shut and headed straight for Blue. He could care less about the cop that pulled Blue over. If he's brave enough to get out of his car when these bullets start flying, then he deserves to be shot, he thought to himself as he rounded the corner where Blue was.

It must have been luck tilting in Blue's favor, because by the time Villain got around the corner, Blue was pulling off and out of shooting range.

Villain darted back to his car, throwing the M-16 in the back seat and pulling off, praying that he didn't lose Blue. For a minute he thought he did, until he spotted the S.550 a block away.

The cop car that pulled Blue over was now behind Villain, and when the cop car's lights came on, the first thing that came to Villain's mind was to pull over as quickly as possible, jump out, fire about 25 shots into the cop car and keep it moving until he caught up to Blue. This was about to happen, but it didn't because the cop car went around Villain's car and proceeded to get on the expressway.

Villain sped up, catching up to Blue at a red light. He was about two cars behind him. City workers were doing some work on the street so the traffic was moving very slowly in all directions. But this didn't matter to Villain. He grabbed the M-16 from the back seat, put the car in park, and jumped out with the large gun in both hands.

People in their cars looked on in amazement at this man walking in between cars with a huge gun. Some thought he might be a police officer, and others thought he might be a terrorist. Either way, they got the chance to see Villain do his thing.

Villain raised the gun as if he had some type of military training and walked right up to the driver's side window of the Benz.

Blue turned to look, only to see the long barrel of the M-16 pointed directly at his face. Fearless, he rolled his window down, hoping to get a few words in before Villain pulled the trigger, but was only greeted by the first shot that ripped through his stomach, causing him to step on the gas. The Benz crashed into the car that was in front of him, shutting his car engine off and ejecting . the air bag.

"Come on, Villain! Let me live!" Blue managed to get out with his mouth full of blood. "I got ya money and the drugs."

"Fuck you, Blue! Take it to hell with you and see if you can buy your way into heaven," Villain shot back. He raised the gun up to Blue's face and squeezed the trigger. With the gun on fully automatic, the rapid fire knocked sections of Blue's face and head all over the inside of the car. Brain fragments splattered on Villain as well, given the fact that he was within two feet of Blue and basically firing at point blank range. There wasn't a bullet that didn't hit Blue.

The people in the surrounding cars did their best to get as far away from Villain as possible by backing up and driving on the sidewalk to get around the car. Those who were in front of Blue ran the red light, which caused a few minor fender benders.

Villain tossed the M-16 onto Blue's lap, ran to his car and peeled off, side-swiping a few cars during his getaway. The entire time he was speeding away from the scene, he kept a mischievous smile on his blood-spattered face. It was the moment he'd been waiting for, ever since Blue kicked him in the ass. It was this moment he would cherish during the ride back to Philly.

Codwell, Grant, the district attorney, the witness and Cindy's lawyer McMonigal all stood in for the line-up.

McMonigal couldn't believe that Detective Codwell had found the crackhead who had witnessed Cindy jump into the truck on 13th Street. Today would be the determining factor of whether or not Cindy would be charged with the murders.

Six women walked into the room and lined up side by side. Cindy was number three. She was still wearing the same clothes she had on yesterday, and since then she wrapped her hair is ago when the murders occurred.

The crackhead, whose name was Pam, looked through the one-way glass window at the women, and locked her eyes on Cindy almost instantly.

"Do you see the woman who got into the white SUV on 13th Street?" Detective Codwell asked, standing close to her as a form of intimidation. "She got out of the car with the two dead bodies, then jumped into a white SUV," Codwell continued. "You don't have to be afraid. Nobody can see you from back there."

"Are you going to let her pick, or are you going to pick for her?" McMonigal chimed in; breaking the trance that Codwell had Pam in.

Pam stared at Cindy, and even though the glass separated them, it looked like Cindy was staring right back at her. Pam wasn't afraid of Cindy. It was just the code of the streets kicking in that made her think twice about identifying her.

Pam began to think about the risks and benefits of not picking her out. Pam was sure she would find Cindy and collect a good chunk of money for helping her out. On the other hand, if she did point her out she would probably get killed before she was able to testify against her. The law officials always say that they would protect a witness, but they never do a good enough job, and Pam was well aware of that.

"I don't see her," Pam said, taking her chances with Cindy rather than with the detectives. "The girl is not in there. Can y'all bring in some more women?" she said, playing stupid.

McMonigal looked at the District Attorney. "Can my client and I leave now? It's clear that the only evidence that Detective Codwell has, has shown to be no evidence at all. If you let us leave now, I give you my word that I won't file a lawsuit against the police department for detaining my client for no apparent reason," he said, sending legal threats toward the DA.

The DA had no other choice, but to release Cindy right then and there. Codwell and Grant were hot. They hated to see Cindy leave while knowing in their gut that she was the perp. Without a suspect, they had no case, and without any witnesses willing to stand up, it would be a bumpy ride to a conviction in a court of law.

Cindy walked out of the police station and was met by McMonigal and her cousin, Hassan. A feeling of relief that she couldn't explain shot through her. For a moment, she thought she was finished when the detectives told her that they had a witness who could identify her, along with the fact that Rick was busted in the truck that was full of bullet holes from the shootout. The cards seemed to be stacked against her.

"Didn't I tell you to relax?" McMonigal said to her while proudly poking his chest out as if he actually did any work.

"Yeah… So I guess it's over?" she asked.

"For now, but I have to tell you, that woman who came to identify you, knew exactly who you were, Cindy. I looked at her and she was looking right at you. The detectives knew that she knew who you were, too."

"Well, why didn't she pick me out?"

"I don't know, but you got lucky," he said, opening his car door. "Look, I have to go check on Rick right now. I'm trying to see if I can at least get him out on house arrest until he goes to trial. Call me a little later so I can let you know what's going on with him."

"Alright, tell Rick I'll probably be over to see him tomorrow and to keep his head up."

Villain walked into the club to see Christina and Mike sitting in one of the V.I.P. booths. She looked like she was crying all morning. Mike just sat there with his head down low, barely making eye contact.

The first thing Villain thought was that something happened to Tazz because he never saw Christina cry. "What's going on? Why all the long faces?" he asked, praying that his best friend wasn't in any danger.

"Tazz called here about an hour ago. He told me to tell you to be here the next time he calls," Mike responded.

"Alright, so why the long faces?" he asked again, seeing that there had to be more to it than just waiting for a phone call.

"I know my husband, Villain, and something is wrong. I can hear it in his voice. I tried to call his phone back, but it was off. I swear, I know something is wrong," Christina said, starting to cry all over again.

She was crying so much that it made Villain upset. Tazz was his right hand man, and if anything bad happened to him, it would crush him.

When Christina's phone started to ring everyone looked at the phone sitting on the table simultaneously. Villain snatched it from off the table and answered. "Yo, who dis?"

"Damn, bro! Where the hell have you been?" Tazz asked, happy to hear Villain's voice. "We got a problem."

"What's going on, Tazz? You got ya wife here crying. She said something was wrong wit' you—"

Tazz cut him off. "I need you to grab 100 chickens and drop them off for me," he said, referring to 100 bricks of cocaine.

Drake stood over Tazz while he was talking to Villain and giving him instructions. Tazz was smart, but Drake was smarter. Plus, he was one step ahead of him.

The gun being pressed up against Tazz's head made it hard for him to concentrate.

"Tell him to bring everything," Drake instructed Tazz, while pressing the gun harder up against his head.

Tazz had already hung up the phone, which was the worst thing he could have done. The butt of the gun knocked Tazz off the bed, which caused a one-inch gash on his head, and blood instantly poured down the center of his forehead. He didn't even have time to recuperate from the first blow when the second one broke his nose and knocked two of his front teeth out.

Peaches put her hands over her face, cringing at the sound of Tazz's face being split wide open.

Drake was sending a clear message that he wasn't going to play too many games. "Are you going to play by my rules, or am I going to have to break every bone in ya face in order to get what I want?" he threatened Tazz while standing over him.

"Fuck you, nigga! Ya gonna have to kill me!"

Drake leaned over Tazz, chuckling at the thought of him being rebellious. "Now, why would I kill you?" he asked hypothetically. "Look, we can do this the easy way, and you might end up leaving out of here alive... or we can do it the other way. But I need you to truly understand that if we go the other route, I promise you that your body won't be able to handle the pain I'm capable of inflicting. I'm not telling you this to try to scare you. I just want to give you an option."

Looking up at Drake with blood still flowing from his head and mouth, Tazz thought about everything he was saying. It wasn't really worth being a 'gangsta' in this situation. The best thing for him to do, which he well knew, was to comply. Although Tazz portrayed himself as a gangsta on the outside, deep down in his heart he wasn't ready to die; especially at the hands of someone like Drake. He had a little over seven million stashed in his house, two hundred bricks of cocaine in a refrigerator located in the basement of the club, and a million dollars worth of jewelry, some of which was on his neck and wrist right now.

"That option I was telling you about earlier," Drake continued, "you can either go home to nothing and start over from scratch, or you can die with everything, and watch me from hell while I kill everybody you love, burn down every piece of property you own, and eliminate your name from off the face of the Earth." He held the cell phone in front of Tazz's face.

Tazz didn't think twice. He grabbed the phone and dialed Christina's number, having it answered on the second ring. He looked at Drake once more, and then took a deep breath, swallowing a mouth full of blood. Tazz decided to take the first option, because he wanted to live.

Chapter 15

Cindy took the Broad Street subway train downtown so that she could make it to the bail hearing scheduled for Rick. Public transportation was the only way she was getting around, due to the detectives that would follow her anywhere she went if she was driving. It would be harder to keep up with me if the detectives had to catch the train or bus. She thought to herself about how different she felt riding the bus, and how it was just a few years ago that this was her only mode of transportation.

With Hassan by her side, she walked into the courtroom dressed in a pair of jeans; a white T-shirt and Gucci flip flops.

Hassan drew a lot of attention, wearing a full-length white thobe, a white kufi and a pair of black leather Kuffs; the attire of a true believing Muslim from overseas. His beard reached down to the center of his chest, and the

JOY DEJA KING AND CHRIS BOOKER

scent of imported green musk prayer oil suffocated the courtroom when he entered.

McMonigal, Rick's lawyer, was already in the courtroom and only had a brief moment to explain to Cindy what was going to take place.

It was pure coincidence that Rick's probation officer knew McMonigal and had so for a number of years, given the fact that she and McMonigal dated briefly right after they both graduated the same year from college. It was a good thing that the relationship between the two remained friendly. It was only because of their career choices that they decided not to pursue a committed relationship. They remained friends throughout the years, which led to the favor McMonigal asked of her.

"All rise!" the court clerk announced, coming from out of the judge's chamber with the judge in tow.

The proceedings began with the District Attorney objecting to Rick being released on bail when he was in violation of his probation by getting arrested. The long list of prior arrests and two felony convictions boosted the DA's argument that Rick should not be released from jail until he stood trial for eluding the police and taking them on a high-speed chase around the city. The argument was strong and sound, until it was McMonigal's turn to speak.

"Your Honor, under the United States Constitution, my client is innocent until proven guilty in a court of law," McMongial began, with his left hand in his pocket and an ink pen in the other. "What's clear here, Your Honor, is that my client's bail was set at $150,000. The only reason he hasn't made bail was because he has a detainer for a probation violation from this court. I spoke to his probation officer, Ms. Gill, who said she doesn't have a problem with releasing my client. He paid all of his fines and restitutions. He attended and completed anger management. He never had dirty urine, nor was he ever late or absent from any court hearings in the past."

The DA looked over at the probation officer, Ms. Gill in disgust, thinking that she should have been on his side instead of McMonigal's.

When the judge asked her for an opinion, she just agreed to everything McMonigal said. What else could she do? He was only telling the truth. Plus, the payback from this favor could be very beneficial, Gill thought to herself.

After hearing both sides, the judge took a brief recess in order to make his decision.

"So, what's going to happen now?" Cindy asked McMonigal, satisfied with the way he was handling the case.

"Well, the judge will be back in a minute with his ruling. I think the detainer will be lifted until the outcome of the trial. If the judge gives him house arrest, does he have a place to stay?" McMonigal asked.

"Yeah, he has somewhere to go. You think we run the streets all day just to be homeless at the end of the night?" Cindy asked jokingly.

"All rise!" the clerk said, reentering the courtroom and cutting Cindy and McMonigal's conversation short.

Cindy didn't even have time to ask McMongial why Rick wasn't in court. She didn't know that the proceedings could go on without him being there. She expected to see him, and for him to see that she was there for him the way a real friend should be.

McMonigal never got the chance to explain to Cindy that it was his choice not to have Rick present for the hearing because he knew from experience that the judge would most likely rule against the defense just because Rick was big, black and looked like a gangsta.

"My better judgment tells me not to allow Mr. Johnson to be released today, but because he's presumed innocent until the government proves otherwise, I'm inclined to allow him to post bail," the judge began. "What I will stipulate is that Mr. Johnson be put on house arrest until trial. Does council have a problem with that?" the judge asked.

McMonigal and the DA shook their heads, indicating that house arrest wouldn't be a problem.

Cindy looked on. Her money was well spent by hiring McMonigal not only as her personal attorney, but also to represent anyone she asked him to. Even though Rick would be out on house arrest, she still needed him for a number of reasons; and if push comes to shove, Rick would go on the run before he went back to jail.

The drop-off was supposed to be at a recreational center on 55th Street near Christian Street in West Philly. Drake sent Peaches to pick up the goods so that he could keep an eye on Tazz.

This was nothing new to Peaches, and she was more than willing to regain Drake's trust, because in all actuality she still loved him. Tazz was beginning to have an effect on her, and given more time, she probably would have chosen him over Drake. But for now, Drake had two things that Tazz didn't have: one being history, and the second being a gun. It wasn't hard to make the decision who she was riding with after Tazz's dick could no longer cloud her judgment.

Peaches pulled up to the rec center in Drake's rental car. The black Escalade truck he described was waiting there with the headlights off. She knew someone was in the truck because smoke was coming from out of the exhaust pipe. She beeped the horn twice as instructed by Drake, and out from the truck came two men. One was armed with a large assault rifle, while the other one went to the back of the truck. Peaches became instantly scared, thinking that Tazz's people were just going to kill her out of anger.

Bold, but scared as hell, Peaches grabbed the .40 caliber from under her seat and pulled right up next to the truck. She didn't have to say or do anything, but pop the trunk so the men could put the drugs and money into it. This was all part of the plan Drake had designed to make the drop successful.

Within minutes the trunk of the Crown Vic was loaded and the sounds of two taps on the trunk indicated that the men were finished and she could pull off. Her gun remained clutched, cocked, and ready for action the entire time.

The sun was setting and the night was beginning to darken the sky when Peaches pulled out of the rec center. So that no one would be able to follow her without being seen, she took a route that only she and Drake were familiar with. The normal drive back to her apartment would take about a half hour, but with the route she was taking it would take a little more than one and a half hours, including a number of curves and turns most SUVs would be unable to make.

She grabbed her cell phone from the center console. A quick call was all she could make because she wanted to avoid getting pulled over by the cops with all the stuff in her car. "Yo, I got it," she said to Drake when he answered his phone. "I should be there in a couple of hours."

"Look, before you get on the expressway, I want you to pull over and check to see what they gave you. You don't have to count it, just tell me what it looks like," Drake instructed. He was sitting in a chair with his gun in his hand, staring at Tazz who was sitting on the floor holding a rag over his bloody mouth.

Peaches immediately pulled over into a gas station, got out of the car and did a thorough scan of the cars that came into the gas station behind her. The SUV at the rec center was nowhere in sight.

She popped the trunk and took a quick inventory, giving Drake a description of what she was looking at. "I see four very large black duffel bags, and two smaller duffel bags. The small bags have money in them, and the large bags have the coke in them," she told Drake as she quickly unzipped and zipped each bag.

"Alright, you did good. Come on home," he said, then hung up the phone.

Peaches closed the trunk and took a good look around once again before getting back into the car. She was still pretty nervous from the drop at the rec center, and knew for sure that she wasn't in the clear yet.

Sometimes being too nervous could be a bad thing, and in this case Peaches' nerves caused her not to notice the dark blue car that began following her when she pulled out of the gas station. Because it wasn't the SUV she saw at the rec center, she didn't pay the raggedy little Honda any attention. If she had any idea whatsoever that Villain had a plan of his own concerning the kidnapping of his best friend, and the fact that it was him in that little blue car following her, she would have thought twice about the role she was playing in this score. She was in too deep. As far as Villian was concerned, she was the mastermind of it all, and killing her would be just as easy as killing any other nigga on the streets who tried to pull this kind of stunt.

Villain wasn't new to the game, so he was well aware that she wouldn't be going directly back to where Tazz was, so it was the patience game that would make him successful in finding Tazz, or at the least finding out where all the goods were going.

He kept a nice distance behind Peaches, avoiding an obvious tail every time she checked her rearview mirror. Villain had a full tank of gas, and the car he was driving had four cylinders, which meant that he could follow her until she had to refill her gas tank or until she made it to her destination. Either way, whenever she did stop, he was going to push forward with what he had planned.

Memories of growing up with Tazz flooded his thoughts. This caused him to become highly enraged, and he thought about all of the diabolical things he was going to do to the people who were responsible for the kidnapping of his best friend.

Chapter 16

After court, Cindy headed back to South Philly to meet up with a guy who could possibly be her new connect for purchasing large amounts of cocaine. D-Rock, Cindy's old-head, set the meeting up a couple of days ago after she inquired about where and who her father used to cop his drugs from back in the day. She had told D-Rock her plans of taking over all of Philadelphia as opposed to just South Philly, and how she was looking for a new supplier with good coke for cheap prices. D-Rock was well out of the game, but he still knew people that knew people who knew of a guy that could meet her needs in the drug game.

It wasn't long before Cindy pulled into the Pathmark parking lot on Grays Ferry Ave. The parking lot wasn't where the meeting was to take place, but rather in the dairy aisle of the supermarket.

When she got to the aisle, the only people there were an old lady putting milk in her shopping cart, another woman grabbing some Lunchables for her small child, and a stock boy refilling the ice cream freezer. "What kind of bullshit is this?" Cindy mumbled under her breath, taking a look at her watch to make sure that she was on time.

"Ma'am, you look lost. Can I help you with anything?" the stock boy asked, not taking his eyes off of the ice cream he was stocking.

"No, I'm fine," she shot back with an attitude.

The boy chuckled at the way she answered him back. He stood up, now focusing his eyes on Cindy. The voice of a young boy disappeared and was replaced with a stern, but not too deep, Hispanic accent. "You know, I'm willing to bet my last dollar that ya name is Cindy," he said, opening up the icebox in front of where she was standing in order to stock more milk.

"Who the fuck are you and how do you know my name?"

"I'ma have to talk to D-Rock about ya nasty mouth," he said in a joking way. "My name is Carlos. We were supposed to meet to discuss some business. D-Rock set it up."

"Oh shit! I'm sorry. I didn't know. D-Rock didn't tell me that you worked here." It took her by surprise that her future connect was stocking food in a supermarket. She expected someone different. Carlos may have had the best cover she had ever seen before in her life.

"What kind of weight are you tryin' to buy?" he asked, still continuing to stock the icebox with milk.

"I want to start off with a couple bricks just so I can see what kind of product I'ma be buying."

"A couple bricks?" Carlos asked, insulted by the amount she was requesting. "If all you want is a couple of bricks, you can go to Max's pizza shop and get that."

The sound of Max's name coming from his mouth was in itself an insult to her. She didn't know that Carlos was bigger than what she thought he was. It was Carlos who supplied Max and almost everybody else in the city that was getting a lot of money. The stock boy position at the supermarket made Cindy underestimate his capabilities. Carlos closed the icebox and was ready to leave.

Cindy had a feeling that the guy was the truth and didn't want to miss out on a good opportunity. "Alright, how much are you going to charge me for 100 bricks of powder?" she said, getting Carlos' attention as he was about to walk away.

He paused for a moment, then opened up the icebox door again and began stocking milk. "See, I knew you wouldn't make D-Rock out to be a liar," he said with a grin as he stocked. "Look, I only produce the best cocaine, Cindy. You want grade-A coke, I got it for you. If you want grade-A heroin, I got it."

He took in a deep breath and exhaled. "I'll give you 100 bricks of cocaine, grade-A, for 12-k a brick, which includes delivery to your front door. The more we do business, the cheaper the coke gets. Cash on delivery, and make sure you're at the place of delivery at the correct time. If my guys got to travel through the city with 100 bricks of cocaine and you're not there to make the buy, I will never do business with you again. I wouldn't care if you wanted 500 bricks. I don't front out cocaine, so please don't ask me. If you ever try to give me funny money or try to rob me, I will kill you, come to your funeral and kill everybody who attends the viewing. I'm not tryin' to disrespect you, but you're from the streets, so you should understand where I'm coming from."

He broke everything down to Cindy, and she could do nothing, but respect what he was saying, especially about passing him funny money or trying to rob him. Her consequences would be the same if someone tried to do that to her. It was all part of the game, and she was familiar with the rules.

"When is the earliest you can make the delivery?" she asked, whipping out her cell phone to get Carlos' information.

"Put ya phone up," he said, seeing she had taken it out. "I get off work in 45 minutes. I'll call you in one hour, exactly."

Peaches entered the apartment, breaking the silence in the room as Drake sat in a chair, while Tazz remained on the floor in the same place he was when she had left. On her shoulder was the smaller duffel bag that contained the cash, and in her hand was a .40 caliber. She walked into the bedroom and tossed the money onto the bed before heading to the bathroom.

Drake looked at Tazz, smiled, and got up to empty out the contents of the bag. "Damn, boy! It looks like ya people came through for you this time," he said, clapping two wads of money together that he just pulled out of the bag.

"Alright, you got what you wanted, so be a man of your word and let me go."

Drake wasn't paying Tazz any mind. He heard what he said, but the decision that he was going to die before it was all over with was already made when Drake first walked through the bedroom door and saw him fucking Peaches. It was pointless just to kill Tazz out of anger when it was already established that Drake was going to rob him for the two hundred bricks of cocaine in the first place. Catching him with Peaches just made things worse.

Peaches walked out of the bathroom just in time.

Drake sat down in a chair, patted his thigh and said to her, "Come sit down, baby girl."

She complied, taking a seat on his lap. When she sat down, a strange feeling came over her when Tazz looked up at her with a bloody face.

"Tell me something, Peaches. Do you love this nigga?" Drake asked, pointing his gun at Tazz.

She didn't hesitate for one second before the word "no" came out of her mouth. It was true. She didn't love Tazz, and it wasn't because Drake had a gun in his hand and murder in his eyes. She hadn't known Tazz long enough to love him, but she did have strong feelings for him. The man she did love was Drake, but at this point she didn't know if Drake still loved her back.

Drake wrapped his arms around Peaches, slipping the gun into her hand. "Do you still love me?" he asked her while staring into Tazz's eyes.

"Come on, Drake," she said nervously.

"Answer me!" he yelled.

"You know I love you, Drake. Don't be stupid."

"Well, if you love me, I want you to kill him. I want you to shoot dis nigga in his head. If you do, I'll forgive you and we can go back to doin' what we do."

Hearing that, Peaches raised the gun and pointed it directly at Tazz's face. Her reaction wasn't in accord with her heart. Her heart was telling her not to take a life, but she had gone too far to turn back now.

The room became silent for a moment before Tazz started begging Peaches not to shoot him. With his arms tied behind his back and his legs tied together, all he could do was cry as he pleaded for his life.

The pleas started to have an effect on Peaches, who was beginning to lower the gun, but she quickly raised it back up when she heard Drake's voice. "Shoot 'im! Shoot 'im!" he yelled. He was becoming angry at the thought of Peaches having any kind of feelings for Tazz.

Everything began to move in slow motion for Peaches. She could feel her heart jumping out of her chest and the palms of her hands were becoming sweaty. She looked at Tazz, closed her eyes, and squeezed the trigger. The bullet hit his upper right chest, knocking his body to the floor. He was in pain, but still alive.

Drake snatched the gun from out of Peaches' hand, pushed her off of his lap and stood up. "Take the money and go wait in the car," he said, giving her the duffel bag she brought in with her. She complied, taking the bag and running out of the apartment like a bat out of hell.

Drake turned his attention back to Tazz, who was lying on the floor bleeding to death. He stood over Tazz with the gun pointed directly at his face. "Any final words?" Drake asked, hugging the trigger of his gun.

"I just don't want a closed casket," he requested, hoping that Drake wouldn't shoot him in the face.

Drake lowered the gun from Tazz's face and pointed it at his body.

Pow! Pow! Pow! Pow! Pow! Pow! Pow!

All seven shots ripped through Tazz's body at close range, hitting everything from his abdomen to his neck. Drake turned away and walked out of the apartment with the gun still in his hand.

"Shhhhh! Bitch, if you even breathe too heavy, I'ma blow ya fuckin' head off," Villain said as he walked up behind Peaches while she was trying to get the car keys out of her pocket. "You slimy bitch, I knew you had something to do with this shit," he said. He patted her down for a weapon and took the bag from off of her shoulder. "Is Tazz in there?" he asked, grabbing a handful of Peaches' hair and shoving her towards his car that was parked on the other side of the parking lot.

Peaches didn't say a word, but she flinched from the pain of having her hair pulled. The walk back to his car seemed to take forever, and for a moment she wished she had the .40 cal. that she left in the bathroom of the apartment. She wanted to scream out to Drake, but she knew that Villain was serious about blowing her head off if she said a word. In the blink of an eye, she found herself gagged, restrained with zip ties, and thrown into the back seat of Villain's car.

Drake walked out of the apartment and headed for the stairs. When he got to the end of the hallway right before the staircase, he felt the hairs on his arms stand up, which normally meant that something was about to happen. He pulled out the .40 caliber that Peaches left behind, and then cautiously stuck his head out over the stairwell to see if anybody was coming up the steps. Nothing! No one was there.

He looked out of the stairwell window that gave a view of most of the parking lot and saw that his car was empty. Where the fuck is Peaches at? he thought to himself as he began walking down the steps quickly.

Drake stopped on the third floor because he heard the entrance door open then shut. He looked over the rail to see who was coming up the steps. Again, nothing! The situation was starting to become like a horror scene from a scary movie.

Drake got to the bottom of the steps and pushed the exit door open, still clutching the .40 caliber in his right hand. Suddenly, he felt the vibration of his cell phone going off in his pocket. Thinking that it might be Peaches, he hurried to answer it. He looked down at the phone when he took it out of his pocket, and just as he had hoped, it was her. "Where the fuck you at?" he asked.

"Look, nigga. You got what you want. Now where's Tazz?" a deep voice calmly replied.

"Who da fuck is this?" Drake shot back and took the phone from his ear and stared at it as if he was face to face with the person on the other end.

"I'ma be the nigga that blows ya fuckin' head off if you don't tell me where Tazz is at."

Drake began taunting Villain over the phone, not knowing that he was a mere fifteen feet away from him. "Tazz is at the White Horse Apartment Complex, 5th floor, apartment number 521. If you hurry, you might be able to hear his last words before he dies," he said jokingly, but also serious; then he hung up the phone.

Drake didn't even have time to unlock his car door before Villain kicked open the same exit door that Drake had just gone through, and began shooting multiple rounds in Drake's direction. Villain could have easily killed him way before the gun battle began, seeing as he had watched Drake pass by him coming down the stairs. Villain was on the second floor the entire time, but he wanted to be sure that Tazz was in the building before he started shooting.

One bullet struck Drake in the left arm, but he didn't hesitate to return fire, forcing Villain back into the apartment building and closing the door behind him.

With a bloody arm, Drake reached into his back pocket and pulled the 9mm he used to kill Tazz with. Although the pain in his arm began to kick in, he fired several shots at the door Villain was behind, leaving holes the size of quarters in it.

Anytime Villain attempted to open the door the shots reminded him that Drake was on the other side.

Villain knew that he didn't have much time before the police would be there, so he made a dash up the steps to the fifth floor.

As Villian passed by one of the staircase windows, Drake could see that he was heading to the apartment in search of Tazz, which gave him more than enough time to get into his car and pull off. If he didn't think that Villain had already killed Peaches, he would have looked around for her before pulling out of the parking lot. To Drake, Villain wasn't the type to leave too many witnesses behind, so he counted her as a dead body.

Villain raced to apartment 521, not knowing what was on the other side of the door before he entered. He didn't know if anyone other than Tazz was in there, so he proceeded with caution.

The bedroom door was slightly open and a pair of legs could be seen on the floor. He opened the door, and saw Tazz, lying there with bullet holes and blood everywhere. He dropped his gun, fell to his knees, and pulled Tazz's lifeless body into his arms. The tears began flowing uncontrollably. His best friend was lying dead right in front of his eyes.

"Come on, baby boy. Don't die on me," Villain said, shaking Tazz's body. He wasn't ready to give up on him so soon. He began giving him mouth-to-mouth and pressing down on his chest, trying his best to give him CPR, which he didn't know much about.

Something he had done worked, because Tazz coughed up a mouthful of blood and he weakly regained consciousness.

Villain quickly held him in his arms again, and Tazz looked at him and smiled before going back out.

With one scoop, Villain lifted Tazz and bolted out of the apartment, hoping he could beat the police sirens in the air a short distance away. "Come on, bro. Stay wit' me," he continued to tell Tazz.

The more he moved, the heavier Tazz's body got, indicating that the very life that was left in him was leaving his body. Even then, that wasn't enough for Villain to give up getting Tazz to a hospital, which he remembered passing not too far down the road. For now, all he could do was watch Tazz die in the back seat of his car, and hear Peaches scream through her duct-taped mouth on the floor below him.

$$\mathcal{C}hapter\ 17$$

Cindy turned one of her low-key crack houses on 29th Street into home base for "Operation Take-Over". The house was crowded with people, while Cindy was in the kitchen cooking up some of the purest cocaine the city had ever had.

After the meeting with Carlos last night, 100 bricks of grade-A cocaine were delivered to her front door, just as Carlos promised. Cindy, who was a whiz when it came to math and money, mathematically calculated the profit made from this deal. From one brick of powder cocaine, she turned it into sixty ounces of crack by cooking it. Cooking fifty bricks of cocaine into crack, she produced 3,000 ounces, bagging up $1,100 worth in five and ten dollar bags for street sales off of each ounce, which alone equaled $3.3 million.

Then Cindy took 25 more bricks of cocaine and turned it into crack for a total of 1,500 ounces that sold for $800 per ounce, making a total of $1.2 million just by selling quarter ounces, half ounces, and whole ounces of crack to local corner drug dealers.

With the last 25 bricks of powder cocaine, she sold it by the brick at 18k per brick. She only made close to a half million, but the whole idea of that was to build up her clientele for large buyers.

All together she would see about $5 million off of 100 bricks of cocaine, minus the $1.2 million she paid. The profit was in the range of $3.8 million.

With 15 workers, each one would get paid at the end of the month, bringing home 20k if all the cocaine was sold by then, i.e., the crack that was bagged up for street sales.

Everybody played a position, and even though Rick was on house arrest, he too played a major part by collecting, counting and making sure all the drug money from the numerous crack houses in South Philly was accounted for. His job was kind of easy, seeing as he didn't even leave the house.

While Cindy was in the kitchen cooking up the cocaine, five workers sat at the table in the dining room, weighing and bagging up ounces and quarter ounces of crack. Over in the living room, five more workers sat at another table, bagging up nickel and dime bags. Everybody was busy, including two workers who stood out front and on the roof with Mac-90 assault rifles, securing not just the house, but the entire block.

Inside, it looked like an assembly line, and just for that one day, bagging and tagging was the mission. Like the boss that she was, Cindy compensated everyone lovely for their time. The workers that were bagging up weight were paid $100 an hour, seeing as the 12 by 12 ziplock bags were hard to open and stuff with crack because of how small they were. The workers often complained about how their hands were cramping up, but time was money so they quickly adjusted to it.

Cindy was definitely about to flood the whole city with cocaine powder and crack. She was sure that there would be a lot of bumps in the road ahead of her, especially trying to take over the north side of Philly where it's rumored to be the hardest. Plus, the fact that she was a woman wouldn't make things any easier. Little did the city know, she went harder than most of the men who are supposed to be some of the top dogs running around with multiple bodies under their belts, and with money stacked to the ceiling. It's really a man's world when it comes to the drug game in Philly, but every now and again a change comes along and puts a twist to the game. At this moment, Cindy put in too much work and came too far to choke up now. It was either go hard or go harder.

Detective Grant almost tripped over his feet running into the office where Detective Hill was sipping on his morning coffee. They were still the lead detectives on the Broad Street bar shootout where one man was killed and several others wounded.

Grant was excited to break the news to Hill about the anonymous tip that came in via telephone this morning. "You're not going to believe this," he said, tossing a small piece of paper in front of Hill. "Our girl, Cindy, hasn't been telling us the truth lately. Do you remember a couple of years ago when the city was pretty much under siege by those Russian chicks who were running around killing everything moving in search of those diamonds?"

Hill thought for a moment. "Oh yeah, I remember, but what do the Russians have to do with Cindy?" he asked, wanting to know where Grant was going with all of this.

"It's not the Russians I'm talking about. Remember the three bank robbers who started all of that mess? Chase, Rolex, and ah... ah... what's that other guy's name?" Grant asked, snapping his fingers.

"Blaze or Blade... something like that."

"Yeah, Blade. Now, do you remember when Rolex had that big shootout with the police in South Philly?"

"Yeah, go on."

"He had a girlfriend with him that nobody could identify because of all the bullets that she and Rolex were shooting out of the window. Well, I got a tip this morning that Rolex's girlfriend's name was Erica Willborn. After Rolex was killed, she had a baby by him, stayed in the city, but changed her name to Cynthia McParson for safety reasons. I checked out the story and it was true. Cindy is really Erica!" Grant went on to tell Hill.

Hill sat back in his chair. It all made sense to him, but the only problem was that they didn't have enough evidence to charge Cindy with the police shooting, or any other shootings for that matter.

Both Hill and Grant were angry at the thought of Cindy walking around freely after she could have possibly been the one who killed the officer during the police shootout that she and Rolex were involved in a couple of years ago. Then, the fact that she's a suspect in a number of present-day murders only made things worse. In every case, there was never a witness, or at least a witness who wasn't afraid to identify her as the shooter.

"Well, I guess we've got our work cut out for us," Hill said, rising to his feet.

"Yeah, but we got to get some concrete evidence on her, because if we don't, her lawyer is going to eat us for breakfast," Grant said, walking out of the office with Hill in tow.

"Wake up, you dumb bitch!" Villain yelled, bringing Peaches out of her sleep.

The sight of Villain immediately brought tears to her eyes. She was still bound and gagged so she couldn't yell or scream; not that it would have mattered considering where she was. She looked around and nothing was familiar to her. All she could see was the moon and the stars in the night sky. It appeared that she was on a roof of some sort.

Her thoughts were confirmed when Villain grabbed a handful of her hair and lifted her to her feet—tipping half of her body over the edge of the roof. The distance between her and the ground was 18 stories high, as most project buildings were in Philly. She tried to scream but nothing came out because her mouth was still duct-taped.

"You're going to tell me everything I wanna know, or ya ass better know how to fly!" Villain said, jerking her over the edge. "Do you understand?"

Peaches couldn't nod her head any faster while agreeing to his terms. To her, being thrown off of an 18-story building would probably be the worst death in the world. She would rather be shot than die that way.

"If you scream, I'm throwing ya ass over," Villain said, snatching the tape from her mouth. "Who set this shit up?"

"Please don't kill me!" Peaches begged.

Villain just jerked her body further over the edge. "Answer the fuckin' question. Who set this shit up?"

"My boyfriend. It was my boyfriend, Drake." She began talking a mile a minute, telling Villain everything that she knew. She told him about Drake and Veronica taking the money out of Tazz's bank account. She told him how Drake told her to keep Tazz busy while they did it. She even told him about the time she was eavesdropping on the conversation about the 200 bricks of cocaine Villain and Tazz had at the club the day Blue robbed him.

Villain had to smack her to get her to stop talking so he could ask another question. "Where the fuck is Drake at right now? And bitch, you'd better not lie to me."

"I don't know! I don't know!" Peaches cried out.

Villain jerked her again. She cried out, hoping he wouldn't throw her over. "I can find him! I can find him!" she said in an attempt to negotiate for her life. "I'll find him for you. Please, don't kill me!"

If Villain had any idea of where to find Drake, he would have tossed Peaches over the edge, but he didn't know where he could be or anything about him for that matter. As badly as he hated it, he needed Peaches to locate him. Not only did he want Drake, he wanted any and everybody that had anything to do with the entire situation.

"Bitch, if you're lying to me, you're going to wish I threw ya ass off this building," he threatened, and threw her back down on the roof. "Find him!"

Although Kim was still angry with Drake, being this far into her pregnancy, she thought it best to be home instead of staying with her sister. She waddled down the steps and headed straight for the kitchen. Kim was just about 8 months and it seemed that overnight she blew up; she was eating anything and everything she could get her hands on. She stood in the kitchen with the refrigerator door wide open, debating whether or not she should eat leftover Hamburger Helper or devour a large piece of crumb cake she bought from the supermarket earlier that day. The hell with it! she thought to herself, and then grabbed both of the plates.

It might have been the smell of the Hamburger Helper when she took the Saran Wrap off of the plate that made her feel unusually nauseous. A sharp cramping pain in her stomach followed the nausea, and suddenly her water broke.

She then grabbed the kitchen phone from off of the wall and dialed 911 first. It was 11:30 at night, and all she could think about was where Drake was. She needed him right now. She could barely get the words out to the operator that she was having a baby due to the contractions that seemed to be getting stronger and more frequent.

A sigh of relief came over Kim when the lights from a car pulling into the driveway shone through the living room window. She dropped the phone and headed toward the door, praying that it was Drake. At this point, it didn't matter who it was, just as long as they could drop her off at the nearest hospital.

Swinging the door open, she knew that her prayers were answered when she saw Drake getting out of the car. "My water broke!" she yelled weakly and hardly able to hold herself up.

Drake rushed right over to her, catching her by the arm before she dropped to her knees in pain. His adrenaline had kicked in. He didn't even unload the cocaine and money from out of the trunk of the car. He was just as excited about the birth of his son as Kim was. The only thing that concerned him was that the arrival of the baby was a lot earlier than the both of them had expected.

After getting Kim into the car, Drake's phone began to ring. He really didn't want to answer it, but Peaches' number popped up on the screen, indicating that either she was still alive, or Villain may have been the one calling. Either way, Drake could not ignore it. "What's good?" he said as he answered the phone while getting into the car.

"It's me," Peaches responded. "How the hell you just leave me out there like that?"

Drake froze. He wasn't sure whether to be happy that she was still alive or upset that Villain didn't kill her at the apartment complex. The relationship was pretty much over between the two of them. Even if he wanted to forgive Peaches, he would never be able to get the image of seeing Tazz fuck his bitch out of his mind.

He began to think that if Villain did kill her, it would spare him the stress of going through an emotional breakup with her because he knew how badly she would take it. Besides, after seeing her with Tazz, he really didn't care too much about whether she lived or died. But another part of him did, considering how much time they had been together, and all the things they've done over the years. He had mixed feelings about her, but the fact still remained that she was on the other end of the phone, alive and well.

"Look, I'm on my way to the hospital. Kim's water broke. I'll call you in the morning," he told Peaches in an effort to end the phone call fast before Kim started asking who he was talking to.

Drake didn't get but a couple of blocks away from his house before realizing that he still had the cocaine and the money in the trunk of his car. He quickly came to his senses and busted a U-turn back to the house. As badly as he wanted to see the birth of his son, right now the option of speeding down the highway with a trunk full of coke wasn't an option at all. What good would I be to my son if I'm in jail? he thought to himself while blocking out the sounds of Kim yelling at him.

"Where are you going? Why are you turning around?" She didn't need to know, nor would she understand that what was in the trunk was enough to have Drake locked up in jail forever.

Peaches sat up in the back seat of Villain's car, still tied up and unable to utter a word through her duct-taped mouth. The only time she was allowed to speak was when Villain wanted her to. Now, after she just got off the phone with Drake he really didn't have a purpose for her any longer.

Peaches stared out of the window trying to pinpoint a specific location, but there was nothing. All she could see were trees and an open road with no cars on it. She was scared to death. It was pitch black outside, and Villain made the scene in the car even scarier by mumbling under his breath words that she couldn't understand.

The car came to a complete stop in the middle of nowhere, and by the looks of where she was, Peaches knew that this would be her final resting place. She began crying and saying a silent prayer to herself.

Villain got out of the car, opened the back door and pulled her out by her hair. He threw her to the ground, pulled out his gun and pointed it directly at her face. In a daze, he began thinking about how he held his best friend's lifeless body in his arms, and how personal it would be to kill Peaches, Drake, and Veronica. A bullet to the head was too easy. He didn't want to kill her that way. He slowly lowered his gun and tucked it in his back pocket. The psychotic look on his face made Peaches cringe, and the tears she had cried dried due to the deeper fear of dying.

Villain popped the trunk of his car and grabbed a butterfly knife that was in his gym bag. Without hesitation, he grabbed a handful of Peaches' hair, pulled it back so that her neck was exposed, and cut her throat from ear to ear. He didn't even stick around to watch her die. He got in the car and sped off, leaving her there, bleeding profusely from the neck.

With nobody around for miles, Peaches desperately tried to get out of the hand restraints so that she could apply pressure to her neck in order to stop the bleeding.

Drake and Kim finally made it to the hospital safely and in one piece. Between her contractions, Kim had been on the phone during the entire ride, calling her family and Drake's aunt Jackie to let them know that she was having the baby. This seemed like the moment everybody was waiting for, mainly Drake, who brought along a camcorder to record the birth.

Chapter 18

What seemed like sure death only turned out to be about fifteen minutes of Peaches' being unconscious due to the amount of blood she lost. She woke up slightly dazed, feeling the deep stinging sensation of the wound on her neck. Villain had cut her pretty badly, but he left before he could see that he didn't cut into any main arteries that would cause her to bleed to death.

With her arms still tied behind her back, she felt around on the ground for anything sharp enough to cut through the zip ties she was bound with. She found something that she thought might have been a piece of plastic. It wasn't all that sharp, but she began cutting away at the ties the best way she could. Peaches had a will to live and her determination would make her beat the odds.

It must have taken an extra ten minutes alone just to get a big enough slit in the plastic ties to work with. It took another five minutes after that to actually wiggle out of the restraints. She was exhausted and had to take a minute to get herself together again.

The first thing she did was to take her shirt off and tie it around her neck tightly, adding pressure so the bleeding could stop. She knew that she didn't have long to get out of the woods and get to a hospital before she ended up really dying.

She felt a bulge in her back pocket and reached for it, hoping it was her phone. It was. Villain put it there after she got off the phone with Drake.

"Nine-one-one!" the operator said, giving Peaches a sign of hope that she would make it.

"I don't know where I am... I'm bleeding really bad... Please, help me!" Peaches tried her best to yell into the phone as she followed Villain's tire tracks to the road that got her there.

The Present...

"Can I come in?" Villain asked, in an arrogant tone, as he made his way over to the visitors' chairs. "Let me start off by saying congratulations on having a bastard child."

Villain's remarks made Drake's jaw flutter continuously from fury. Sensing shit was about to go left, Kim attempted to get out of the bed with her baby to leave the room, but before her feet could hit the floor, Villain pulled out a .50 caliber Desert Eagle and placed it on his lap. The gun was so enormous that Drake could damn near read off the serial number on the slide. Kim looked at the nurse's button and was tempted to press it.

"Push the button and I'll kill all three of y'all. Scream and I'ma kill all three of y'all. Bitch," Villian paused, making sure the words sunk in, "if you even blink the wrong way, I'ma kill all three of y'all."

"What the fuck you want?" Drake asked, still trying to be firm in his speech.

"You know, at first, I thought about getting my money back and then killin' you for setting my brother up wit' those bitches you got working for you. But on my way here I just said, 'Fuck the money!' I just wanna kill the nigga."

Deep down inside, Drake wanted to ask for his life to be spared, but his pride wouldn't allow it. Not even the fact that his newborn son was in the room could make Drake beg to stay alive, which made Villain even more eager to lullaby his ass into a permanent sleep.

Villain wanted to see the fear in his eyes before he pulled the trigger, but Drake was a G, and was bound to play that role 'til he kissed death.

Villain could see that, and it made him more eager to kill Drake. He wanted Drake to beg for his life. They stared at each other for a moment in silence. Then Villain rose to his feet, took the safety off of his gun and pointed it in the direction of the new family.

Kim wanted to scream, but she couldn't. All she could do was to wrap the baby up in her arms and brace herself for the impact.

Villain's mind went blank as he squeezed the trigger over and over and over again, first striking Drake in the chest. Another bullet hit Kim in the head, killing her instantly.

With a bullet wound to his chest, Drake used his last bit of energy to try and cover Kim and the baby, but he was riddled with three more bullets to his neck. One of the bullets went straight through and hit baby Derrick in his face, killing him instantly as well.

The room was filled with gun smoke, while doctors and nurses scattered around the outside of the room, trying to get to safety. It was chaotic. People were screaming and babies were crying throughout the delivery section of the hospital.

Villain walked out of the room and tossed the gun in a trashcan on his way out. He walked past people who were lying on the ground and not even attempting to raise their heads to get a look at the culprit.

It wasn't until he got on the elevator that he realized what he had just done: He had killed Drake and his family. It was one thing to kill Drake, but Kim didn't deserve to be held accountable for his actions, nor did baby Derrick.

Doctors quickly rushed into the room where Drake, Kim, and the baby were, pulled them out of each other's arms and tried their best to resuscitate them. Kim and the baby were pronounced dead within a couple of minutes, but Drake somehow regained a weak, but consistent pulse.

Kim and Drake's family members who stayed behind made the scene even worse by yelling and screaming at the doctors and security guards not to give up trying to resuscitate Kim and the baby. The entire situation was tragic, and it was sad that the family members had to be there to witness everything.

Not one set of eyes was dry on that hospital floor, and the sounds of crying flooded the room where Kim and baby Derrick were pronounced dead.

Chapter 19

Cindy strutted into the upscale restaurant dressed exactly how she felt... a rich bitch. She was draped in a Stella McCartney color block, figure-flattering dress with a pair of strappy Giuseppe open toe heels that had a black zipper closure and gold leaf accents. They were literally a walking piece of art. Cindy's blinged out wrist and hand clutched her snakeskin purse. Most would think she was the wife of a rich baller, but actually Cindy was the top baller herself.

She wasn't there to eat though, but rather for an un-scheduled meeting with Max. Cindy had gotten word that this was Max's dinner spot every Thursday afternoon. She also found out that Max wasn't buying as much cocaine in the past that she thought he was, making this meeting inevitable according to the terms of Cindy's "Operation Take Over".

"May I help you, ma'am?" the hostess in the waiting area asked Cindy.

"No, I already have reservations," Cindy responded, walking past the hostess as if she wasn't even there. She headed straight to the back of the restaurant where she could see Max and a few of his boys sitting at a table, eating. From a distance, if you didn't know any better, you might have mistaken Max and his boys to be part of the Italian Mob by the way they had their napkins tucked into the tops of their shirts to prevent any food from falling onto their clothes. They used all the eating utensils in the proper way, and two bottles of wine sat in the middle of the table.

Cindy walked up to the table, but was met by one of Max's guys whose only purpose for being there was for Max's security. She looked him up and down as if he wasn't 6 feet 5 inches tall and weighed 270 lbs. She smiled, looked at Max, and then sat at the table directly behind the one he and two of his guys were sitting. Security continued standing until Max told him to have a seat.

Cindy spun her chair around so that it was facing Max. Max looked angry at the fact that Cindy was interrupting his meal, but she could care less about how he felt. This was business.

"I don't conduct business in public. If you're hungry, place an order at the pizza shop," Max said, and took in a mouth full of food. He thought that Cindy was there trying to buy drugs.

"I'm not here for that, Max," she said, grabbing a napkin from off of her table and leaning back in her chair. "I got a proposition for you."

Max tossed his fork onto his plate. He was irritated by Cindy's presence. "What can you possibly have to offer me?"

"Listen, Max. I hate to be the one who tells you this, but South Philly is under new management. I'm well aware that you're only buying 50 bricks of cocaine a month at about 14k a pop. What I'm offering you is that you buy ya coke from me, and I'll give you the same product for 16k."

"16k!" Max said, laughing at the suggestion. "Why would I want to buy my cocaine from you at 16k when I already have my own connect that charges me less? The math doesn't add up. And who the fuck is telling you my business?" he questioned angrily.

"Just like I said Max, South Philly is under new management—"

"And who the fuck is running it? You?" Max shot back, cutting Cindy off. "Bitch, I should blow ya fuckin' head off right now!" he said, pulling his gun from his waistband and placing it on his lap under the table. "You must not know who you're fucking with. I run South Philly, not you!"

Max was getting loud and started to draw a lot of attention to himself. People in the restaurant noticed the tension in the air, but chose to just mind their own business and continue eating and talking.

Max didn't realize what he had done when he pulled his gun on Cindy. The meeting was now over.

"I guess I can take that as a 'no'," Cindy said, and got up to leave. What she really wanted to do was reach into her purse, grab her gun, and have a shootout right then and there, but there was a time and a place for everything.

Her instincts of a boss kicked in, and she walked out of the restaurant the same way she came in—peacefully.

Cindy was growing day by day. She had matured over the past few months and learned how to use qualities such as patience, dedication, and determination, and she also learned how to think with her head before thinking with her heart.

James and Tate, two of Cindy's workers and well-known gunmen in South Philly sat outside of the restaurant waiting for the green light from Cindy to do what they do best. She gave them a nod before getting into her car. She pulled off knowing what was about to happen, and although the inside of the restaurant wasn't a good place for a gun battle, today was the day that Max would retire for good.

Twenty minutes had gone by since Cindy left the restaurant, and Max still hadn't come out yet. James was getting frustrated and was tempted to just run in there and blow Max's head off in front of everybody. But it was a good thing he didn't get out of the car to do that because Max and his three boys finally exited the building.

The swank area where the restaurant was located in was hardly the place where you would want to have a shootout, mainly because the police were just about everywhere. There had to be a right time and place for James and Tate to make their move, so for starters they let Max and his boys get out of the neighborhood before they did anything.

Drake flatlined twice since yesterday, so the doctors weren't too optimistic about him making it. He lost a lot of blood, and there were still two bullets inside his chest, one which had bruised his spinal cord, but not fully paralyzing him.

His hospital room was under high security and his visitors were limited. One detective remained by his bedside, waiting for him to wake up, even if it was for a moment, just so he could try and get a statement.

"Please, Drake, hold on," his aunt Jackie cried, holding his hand briefly while they transported him upstairs for another surgery.

His mother had died when he was nine years old, and his dad never stayed around long enough to watch Drake grow up, so the only family member he had left in his life was his mother's sister, Jackie.

Drake also had a brother that he never met who lived in West Philly where his dad was originally from. His father had cheated on his mother with another woman back in the day, and his brother was a result of that. He only knew about his brother through rumors, and because people said that they looked alike. So, other than him and his aunt Jackie, Drake only had Kim, and the hopes of starting his own family tree.

That dream was beginning to seem impossible because the doctor said that the next time Drake flatlined, it might be his last, especially considering the fact that one of the bullets still left inside of him was close to his heart. If that alone didn't end up killing him, the surgery to remove the bullet could, if the surgeon made the slightest miscalculation.

Some people say that you see your whole life pass by right before you die, and some people even say that you may see the light. But for Drake, it was neither one. There was just a blank; no memory of anything, no dreams, no voices, no heaven, no hell… nothing. Just pitch black darkness.

James and Tate followed Max all the way back to South Philly where it appeared that they were heading to the pizza shop. The large Suburban truck pulled into the gas station on Grays Ferry Avenue. Max got out of the truck and entered the building to pay for the gas. He was followed by one of his men who made it clear that he was carrying a gun by lifting his shirt as if he was trying to adjust himself.

"Take the two in the truck. I got Max," James said to Tate as they pulled into the side of the gas station that faced away from the cameras.

James and Tate both checked their guns to make sure they had a bullet in the chamber. Tate grabbed the two extra clips from out of the glove box and gave one to James. They both got out of the car and walked around to the front of the building.

As Max and his boy were coming out of the building, Max was the first one to see the gunmen, but it was far too late. When you deal with killers like James and Tate, they are coming full steam. Nothing is rehearsed or planned out. When it's time to move, they work within seconds.

All Max could see and hear were the flames from James' gun and the loud clapping behind it. Max's boy didn't even have an opportunity to pull out his gun. The shots were coming so rapidly that he didn't know whether to stand there or run.

Within two or three seconds, James had fired 10 shots from his Glock .40, hitting Max three times in his upper body and once in the side of his head. Max's boy caught four shots to the upper body and two to his left leg, dropping him straight to the ground.

Tate fired simultaneously into the Suburban, killing the driver instantly with a fatal shot to his temple and wounding the other guy in the back seat.

You could hear the sounds of the two empty clips that James and Tate threw to the ground, and the sounds of the two guns cocking a bullet into the chambers from the second clips.

Everything was happening fast. James ran over to Max and his boy and fired another shot into both of their heads to make sure they were dead. Tate did the same, running over to the truck and firing several more shots into the head and body of the wounded guy in the back seat.

What would seem like forever to some people only lasted about 20 seconds, if that. James and Tate fled the scene, leaving nothing behind alive to tell the story.

Max's days of selling cocaine in South Philly were over, and his death would be the start of something good... at least for Cindy and whoever else was riding on her money train.

Chapter 20

One month later...

The crack house on 23rd Street was back up and running, pulling in about 20 grand a day, even on Sundays. Other houses in South Philly, including one on 30th and Tasker, another on 17th and Christian, and two more between 9th and 5th Streets, were also doing impressive numbers daily, roughly producing anywhere between 10 and 15 grand a day.

Local corner-boy hustlers who stood on the block from dusk 'til dawn also profited from the increase in drugs and the decrease in the prices for them.

South Philly was in a good position. The crime rate was down, and kids could play outside without worrying about getting shot. New, up-to-date cars with banging stereo systems flossed their way up and down the streets. Money was plentiful and everybody was eating good—from the boss all the way down to the look-out boys. Every weekend somebody was throwing a party, and even the corner boys had their chance to show off.

There was only one person at the center of all the prosperity brought back to South Philly, and that was Cindy, The Boss. She owned South Philly, and even though what she was doing was building her very own criminal enterprise, things were actually looking better for that section of the city.

At night she made sure the noise level on every corner was down to a minimum so the 9 to 5 workers could rest peacefully. And by the time they woke up in the morning, the streets would be clean, and there would be no drug selling between the hours of 7 to 9:30 in the morning, and from 2 to 5 o'clock in the afternoon, out of consideration for the children going and coming from school. It was mandatory for all the workers to pay somebody to keep the streets clean, and most of the time they paid crackheads to do the job. Cindy even made time to go around early in the morning to inspect the corners where the drugs were being sold.

Today the sun was blazing, and the humidity made it feel like 105 degrees. Even then, the heat didn't stop the kids from playing in the fire hydrant and chasing each other up and down the street with buckets of water.

Cindy, Hassan, and Rick sat on the steps of the house on the corner of 23rd Street and watched the kids playing while enjoying the cool breeze that came from the water flowing from the fire hydrant. The three of them met every Monday, Wednesday, and Friday just to discuss business. These were also the only days that Rick could get a couple hours out of the house because he was still on house arrest.

"You know, I'm supposed to go to trial next month," Rick said. "McMonigal is talking about taking a deal for 11½ to 23 months in the county jail. He said if I was to lose the trial, I was looking at no less than 5 to 10 years."

"Nigga, you better take that deal!" Hassan shot at him before Cindy could say a word. "It ain't like you got a chance to beat it at trial. They chased you through half of the city for about 20 minutes."

"Hassan is right," Cindy added. "You'll probably do nine months in county. Your commissary account will be through the roof, and you know I'll come see you every week, that is, if none of ya little hood rats don't beat me to the punch. Take it as a lightweight vacation. The one thing you don't want to do is play around and wind up going up state for 5 to 10."

They were both right. It was a wonder that McMonigal got the DA to come down on the plea bargain. Rick was originally offered a 4 to 8 year sentence if he didn't go to trial, but seeing as McMonigal was well known and respected throughout the legal system, he pulled a few strings for a lighter plea.

Even with what Cindy and Hassan were telling Rick, it still didn't make things any better. Until one is put in a situation where he has to volunteer his freedom for any amount of time in a 6 by 9 cell, it would be impossible for anybody to tell a man to go to jail and give up his right to be free.

Rick was snapped out of his deep thoughts when a black Ford Taurus with tinted windows turned onto the street, driving slowly through the water coming from the fire hydrant and pulled right in front of where they were sitting. Not knowing who it was, Hassan and Rick both reached for their guns. It really didn't matter who they were, because without question the car would become Swiss cheese if nobody immediately identified themselves; and that's just what they did.

The driver's side window rolled down and a familiar face stuck his head out. "Damn, playboy! It's me, Mike from Carpenter Street," he said, staring at Rick, hoping to ease some of the tension in the air.

Rick did know him, but not that well. Mike was more of a freelance drug dealer hoping to get his corner back to doing the kind of numbers it did from selling crack back in the day. He worked one of the few corners that Cindy didn't have her product selling on, and it was mainly because it was a hot spot for the police. Nobody in their right mind would risk selling drugs out there, especially in the summertime.

"Yeah, what can I do for you, playa?" Rick asked, not yet ready to take his hand off the gun slumped in his waistband. "As a matter of fact, how about you pull over and get out of the car so we can talk? There are kids in the street."

Mike was hesitant, but he did just that. He was more determined to talk business rather than possibly miss his opportunity by pulling off out of fear. He got out of the car looking and smelling fresh to death, standing at 6ft., and weighing 215 lbs. He was light skinned, and sported a closely shaven beard to match his wavy 1½ inch haircut. He and Rick walked a little further down the block away from Cindy and Hassan, who kept their eyes on both of them.

"Damn, man! You know I'm trying to get Carpenter Street back on the map. I really just need a new connect."

"What do you mean, a new connect?" Rick asked, curious to know who his previous supplier was.

"Oh, I was dealing with the dude, Max, at the pizza shop. You know dat nigga got hit up a while back. I was only buying 4½ ounces of powder off of him a week, but I'm trying to step my game up now, and from what I'm hearing, you're the man I should be hollering at."

Rick just stood there listening to Mike talk a mile a minute about his big money plans. "So, how much money are you tryin' to spend?"

"I got like five grand to my name."

"Alright look. Take my number down, and call me when you get five hundred more dollars, and I'll see what I can do for you. I'm not making no promises, but I'll see what I can do," Rick said, not too optimistic about dealing with Mike, whom he really didn't know like that.

After exchanging numbers, Mike got into his car and pulled off. When it came down to selling small weight like 4½ ounces and whole ounces, Rick did most of those deals, taking some of the weight off of Cindy's shoulders and freeing her up for larger deals with more important clientele. Seeing as Mike was spending a few grand, most likely he would be dealing with Cindy directly instead of getting anything from Rick.

DEA Agent Anthony Pesco and ATF Agent Joshua Lavinski sat in Detective Grant's office, awaiting the arrival of both Grant and Hill.

One of the many problems the city police were experiencing was the increase of drug activity in South Philly due to a woman who was also suspected in several murders, a possible robbery, and most importantly a shooting that involved a police officer getting killed and wounding several others. The problem was that the local detectives or police could never get enough evidence for the DA to prosecute her for anything.

With her hands tied, DA Dynel Abraham turned to the FBI for help. But it wasn't really help she was looking for. Abraham knew that she was turning the case over to a pack of wolves that would stop at nothing to get a conviction.

With harsher sentences for drugs and guns, the feds were the number one reason for the disappearance of young black men in the hood. One could only imagine why the conviction rate was at 97%. Most of the time they would threaten young, immature men with life in prison, or many years close to it so that they would be forced to take a deal in order to avoid having to spend the rest of their lives in prison.

The feds also have a tactic that has been proven to work in almost every case, from the smallest to the largest. That tactic is ratting... telling... snitching... squealing... or whatever other names you can think of. In every case, there was always somebody too weak to stand up on his own two feet like a man, i.e. for all conspiracy drug cases. Most of the time, the feds would never have a case to prosecute if everybody kept their mouths shut, but there's always somebody who you least expect to give you up. Sometimes it can be your own family. You never realize the severity of it until you see the one you had faith in or trusted with some of your most intimate secrets take the stand, raise his or her hand, and swear to tell the truth, the whole truth, and nothing but the truth. Then, they point you out, telling anything and everything they know. It's ugly and it's not fair, but it's the game, and if you're playing the game, then expect for it to eventually play you.

Grant and Hill walked into the office. After the agents greeted them they sat down and got right to business. They told them everything: the Broad Street shooting, the 23rd Street shooting, the two dead bodies on 13th Street, and the increase in drug trafficking in South Philly. They also told them about the four dead bodies at the gas station—one of which was a well-known drug dealer by the name of Max. They explained that they believed Cindy was getting rid of the competition. They even told them about the decrease in violent crimes, such as robbery, assault, carjacking, and even murder.

There was a financial study in South Philly where more money was being spent in local stores, supermarkets, car dealers, and clothing stores than there had been in years. The spending was high, but the taxes on government and city checks were low, meaning a lot of people were working under the table or off the books.

To put the icing on the cake in an attempt to frustrate the agents, Grant told them who Cindy really was, and how she was probably involved in the South Philly police shootout. He knew this would get them interested, because every agent in Philly who was around for the mayhem that took place a few years ago concerning $20 million worth of diamonds, the death of a few federal agents, and the lack of a conviction behind all of it, would make them furious.

"Wait! Wait! So you're telling me that this woman had something to do with that diamond case?" ATF Agent Lavinski asked, scooting up to the edge of his chair so that he could hear Grant better.

"We believe that she was the unidentified woman who was shooting out of the window with her boyfriend, Rolex. But we don't believe she took part in the actual robbery."

"What evidence do you have on that case?" Lavinski asked, hoping that Grant had something.

"That's the problem. We know that she was involved, but we just can't prove it. The person who gave the tip about her true identity did just that; gave a tip, and that's it. He didn't leave a name or a number, and the call came from a phone booth in North Philly.

"So, if we can't get her on the cop shooting, and you got no evidence on any other shooting, what else do you have on this woman?" DEA Agent Pesco asked, chiming in.

"Drugs!" Grant said quickly. "We got word from one of our informants that she now supplies the entire South Philly and parts of Southwest Philly. The informant is getting close to her now."

"Where there are drugs, there are guns," Lavinski said with a smile. "If we play our cards right, maybe we can put her behind bars for the rest of her natural life to make up for all the shootings that we can't get her on. Call your informant and tell him to come in for a meeting."

Chapter 21

Drake could hear the sound of his heart rate monitor beeping in his ear. He was finally coming out of his coma for the first time in a month. He wanted to open his eyes, but he couldn't right away, and when he finally struggled enough to do so, everything was blurry. He opened and closed them several times before they started to adjust.

The last person in the world he thought he'd ever see was sitting in a chair right next to him, looking straight at him with the biggest smile on her face. It was Cindy. She had been to the hospital every other day, and with the permission of his aunt, she left one of her workers there as a bodyguard in case the person who shot him wanted to come back and finish the job.

"Hey, handsome," Cindy said, getting to her feet and grabbing a hold of his hand. "Glad to see you back."

Drake wasn't too happy to be back though. It took only seconds after he had opened his eyes to realize that the shooting wasn't a bad dream, and that Kim and his son were dead. His heavy eyes filled up with tears that he couldn't stop from falling down the sides of his face. His heart began to race from the anger and pain he felt about losing his family. The actual pain from the numerous bullet wounds also started to kick in, and the fact that he couldn't move his legs or wiggle his toes made him believe that he might be paralyzed.

The doctor came into the room after getting the word that Drake had come out of his coma. Drake was still awake, but the morphine had him going in and out of sleep. Rest was what he needed.

The doctor was breaking down a bunch of medical terms, and Cindy had no idea what they meant. "Is he going to be alright?" she asked, concerned about Drake slipping in and out of sleep.

"Well, your friend suffered some potentially fatal shots to his back. It's a wonder he came out of his coma, especially this early."

"Is he going to be alright?" she asked again, only wanting to hear the answer to her question.

"Your friend should be okay. He does have a bruised spine from one of the bullets that entered his back, temporarily paralyzing him from the waist down. I'm going to run a few more tests on him later this week, and if everything checks out he'll be released to one of our rehabilitation centers where he'll have to learn how to walk all over again."

Cindy couldn't do anything, but sit back and wait for the next time Drake woke up so that she could tell him what his prognosis was. She felt like she owed him something for saving her life. If it weren't for him, she wouldn't be alive today, and for her, that was major. The same way Drake stuck around to make sure she was straight, Cindy planned on returning the favor. She sat back down in the chair next to his bed and watched him sleep, waiting until he awoke again.

Peaches sat in the back of the police car, watching and waiting for the police to kick down the door of Villain's last known address, and hoping that they would drag him out on his face, or even better, in a body bag. After getting her throat cut and watching the story about the hospital shooting on the news, she went to the police about Villain. She told the cops everything about him kidnapping her and cutting her throat, and she even lied about him being the one who shot Tazz in her apartment.

She gave police another story about how Villain was her ex-boyfriend, and how he vowed to kill anybody she was dealing with, including a guy she was currently dating by the name of Derrick a.k.a. Drake, who may have been his last victim in the hospital shooting. She identified Villain from the surveillance footage from the hospital that was also broadcast over the news for the past few weeks, in hopes that somebody knew who Villain was.

The bottom line, Peaches wanted Villain either dead or put in jail for the rest of his life.

"Search warrant!" the police yelled out after kicking down the front door of Villain's Upper Darby house,

just five minutes from the southwest part of Philadelphia.

SWAT swarmed through the house with large assault rifles, clearing each room, only to find that he wasn't
there. The basement, the first floor, the second floor, and
the attic were all searched and cleared within minutes.
The backyard was searched, the doghouse flipped over
and a small shed was torn apart. The pitbull he had back
there was even shot due to his aggression, and the fact
that he charged at one of the officer's full speed after a
warning shot was fired.

Last but not least, they went to search the garage.
Officers didn't have the garage door opener, so they went
through the house to get to it. The first officer that went
into the door was nervous, thinking that Villain might
jump out from behind all the junk he hoarded inside of
the two-car garage. Amongst some of the things in there
was a Dodge Charger, old furniture including a couch,
a loveseat and part of a bedroom set, and a pile of large
black trash bags that had old clothes in them. Villain
could jump from behind any of these items, and seeing as
he was considered armed and dangerous, this intensified
the search.

After they cleared away the trash bags and furniture,
they could see that the windows on the car were tinted so
dark that you couldn't see anything inside.

Looking through the windshield, a rookie officer
could see something moving on the floor of the back
seat. "Don't move!" the officer yelled, raising his gun
to the window and alerting the other police officers in
the garage to the movement he saw in the back of the
car. "Let me see your hands!" he demanded, now tense

and ready to fire at anything looking suspiciously aggressive.

They all circled the car with their guns pointed directly at the windows. One of the officers finally got the garage door open, shining much needed light into the garage.

Through all of the yelling the police did in telling whoever was in the car to come out, they got no answer or cooperation. Wasting not another minute, one of the officers smashed in the back window on the driver's side, and looked inside to see that there was nobody there. He opened the back door, and to his surprise,c a seven-foot Burmese python was slithering around on the floor. Villain had put the snake there to scare off anybody who would attempt to steal his car. The entire house had been cleared, and Villain was nowhere in sight.

Peaches was pissed Villain was nowhere to be found. She would've bet money that he was going to be stupid and put up a fight and force the police to have to kill him. She asked herself where he could be. This was the only place she knew of, and that was because Tazz brought her there once before. Then she thought to herself about the very place no one had searched yet, which was the club.

"Now, all you've got to do is get her to give you a price for the cocaine you're gonna purchase, and then make the transaction," DEA Agent Pesco told Detective Grant's informant as he hooked the mini microphone up to his belt. "Remember, she's gonna be dealing with a lot of people throughout the day, so make sure you get her to speak clearly."

The first buy wasn't going to be for that much because Cindy wasn't used to dealing with the informant, and the FBI didn't want to raise any red flags that would spoil the operation. The feds were the best at what they did, and were also very patient. This technique was called "building your case", which meant that over time they would consistently buy a certain amount of drugs from the suspect until the total amount was enough to prosecute them in a federal court and could lead to a conviction and a possible sentence ranging anywhere from five years to life in prison. The feds were definitely looking for a life sentence in Cindy's case.

Villain got off of the Greyhound with no idea where he was. He'd been riding the bus from state to state, mainly just trying to get as far away from the city as he possibly could.

Lately, he had been feeling guilty about killing Kim and her baby just to get back at Drake. Killing another man was easy to him, and even a female wouldn't bother him that much considering the situation, but killing a newborn child was new to him. He'd never hurt a kid before, and that was what was bothering him the most.

He looked around to see if he could find a sign telling him where he was. Walking into the bus station, he saw two police officers standing by the counter. Looking at their uniforms, he knew exactly where he was; being very familiar with the police of Norfolk, Virginia. Through all of the busses he'd been on and off of, he thought he would be farther than Virginia by now.

He walked up to the counter to buy another ticket heading west, and when he got there one of the state troopers kept staring at him as if he knew who he was.

Not sure of any of the bus schedules, Villain just asked for a ticket to the next state over.

"Will that be cash or charge, sir?" the woman behind the counter asked him.

Villain was standing there, looking nervous. He thought about the fact that he had to pay with cash, and if he went into his pocket and pulled out the large wad of money he had it might grab the attention of the state trooper, who was already staring him down. He reached into his pocket and peeled off a few bills from the wad. He was trying his best to hurry up and get out of the station and onto the next bus before the state trooper got more inquisitive about whom he was. He didn't want to, but if he had to he wouldn't hesitate having a shootout with the police right there in front of everybody. One sure thing was the fact that Villain would go out in a blaze of glory before going back to jail. Luckily for the state trooper, he didn't give Villain a reason to make a scene.

Cindy left the hospital after visiting Drake, and it was pretty much back to business for the most part. Today was going to be busy, considering all the missed calls she had while at the hospital.

Her first stop was to meet up with the guy named Mike that Rick had introduced her to. The block the dude worked was one hell of a drug corner back in the day, and being that Mike was trying to get it up and running again, Cindy definitely wanted parts of it.

When she pulled up to the block, she could see a flow of crackhead traffic that wasn't light at all. She could also see three or four young drug dealers scattered around the place with no sense of discipline. It looked like everybody was doing their own thing, and nobody was worried about the cops or would-be robbers, because nobody paid attention to what was going on outside of the block. These were the many things that Cindy noticed whenever she pulled up to any drug corner she could potentially take over.

In the midst of all this, there was Mike, leading the pack in being unorganized. For at least five minutes he didn't even notice Cindy sitting on the corner of the block. It wasn't until she beeped the horn that he finally made his way over to the car.

"My bad, baby girl," Mike said, opening the passenger door and jumping into her Range.

Before Cindy did any business with anyone for the first time, they had to go through a series of questions so that she could get to know the person a little better; not on a personal level, but more so just in case something was to go wrong during the course of business. That way she'd know where to find them in case she had to kill them, and Mike was no exception. Even though she wasn't fronting him any cocaine, he was still a nigga in her eyes, and niggas in Philly will rob you, trunk you, hold you for ransom, and then kill you, all for the love of money.

"How long have you been around here?" Cindy asked, pulling away from the corner.

"I've been around here for about five years now. My mom just bought a house on Etting Street."

His mother's house being on Etting Street was a lot for him to just come out and tell Cindy. This meant either one of two things, he was lying, or he didn't think Cindy would be much of a threat. Either way, it was beneficial for her to know that, along with other things he told her about himself during the course of them just riding around the neighborhood. He didn't know that Cindy was going to have his story checked out before the day was over anyway.

"So, Rick told me that you were trying to buy some work," she said, not taking her eyes off of the road to even look at him.

"Yeah. He told me the price for nine ounces of powder would run me about $5,500. I asked him if I could talk to you to see if you can come down a little on the price. It's not that I don't have the $5,500, because I do. I'm just trying to get a consistent drug connect that's not going to have the prices through the roof. I'm only buying nine ounces this time, but what happens if I get my money up, which I will, and want to buy a whole brick? Are you going to charge me 22k?"

"Alright, alright, I hear you," Cindy said, cutting him off and seeing something in him that she once had a few years ago. He was a hustler, and with all due respect he was either going to talk the price down to something cheaper, or this would be the first and last time he bought coke off of her paying these kind of prices. Good business was something she didn't want to lose, and from observing Carpenter Street, Mike had the potential to do something big with the right person backing him up. Eventually that right person would end up being Cindy, hands down, with or without Mike's consent.

She ended up charging Mike $4,800 for the nine ounces of powder, which would eliminate Rick's $700 for setting up the deal. Rick wouldn't mind the loss, considering the fact that Cindy would end up taking care of him later on down the line, plus the fact that she was the boss and could do whatever she wanted to do.

Sitting in his wheelchair and looking out of his bedroom window, Tazz took in the sight of the sun setting, and enjoyed the cool breeze that came off of the ocean right in front of his beachfront vacation home in Atlantic City. He was popping pain pills left and right like they were M&Ms, and Christina had to continuously change his bandages and clean his wounds so they wouldn't get infected.

Christina wished that he had listened to her when she told him to stay in the hospital to get the proper care. But he refused to. It took 3½ weeks for Tazz to be in stable condition, and as soon as he came to and was able to talk, the first words he told his wife were, "Get me out of here!"

It was his wish that nobody knew that he was alive right now. He wanted his body to heal before he made his debut back in the streets. Villain wasn't even aware of what was going on yet, but he would be very soon.

Tazz was shot eight times total in the upper body and survived it. Every bullet hurt like hell, but the worst thing Drake could have done was leave him alive, because payback was a must. And because of all the recent drama and near death experience, Tazz was going back to his old ways, the ways that gave him the nickname "Shooter".

The bus Villain was on pulled over slowly on the highway in the rain at 12:30 in the morning. Most of the passengers were asleep, including Villain who took up the back seats of the bus and made it his bed. The flashing red and blue lights flickered in the bus's rearview mirror, waking up a few of the passengers, but not Villain. He had been up for almost 48 hours straight, so as soon as he got a chance to close his eyes, it was over.

One state trooper car pulled in front of the bus, another in the back, and two more pulled up beside it. Every one of the state troopers got out of their cars with guns drawn, searching for Villain.

Earlier while at the bus station, the cashier recognized Villain from the news a few days ago where the Philadelphia police were on a manhunt looking for him. His face was big as day on CNN. The images from the hospital surveillance weren't good enough to identify him, but with the help of Peaches, the Philadelphia police used a jail photo to post on the news.

"How can I help you, officers?" the bus driver asked the police storming onto the bus.

They didn't respond, but just ran past him and headed straight to the back of the bus while looking at every face they passed.

Villain was still asleep when a state trooper nudged his face with the barrel of his gun, waking him up. The first thing he thought about doing and even attempted to do was reach for his gun, but he had second thoughts after the state trooper took the safety off of his weapon and assured Villain that he would shoot him in his face if he moved again.

"Vincent Thomas, you're under arrest," the cop said as he twisted Villain's hands behind his back and put handcuffs on him.

These were the words Villain dreaded to hear, but the sound of the handcuffs tightening up around his wrists was even worse to the ears. It was over. He was through.

It would take a couple of days, but Villain would be transported back to Philadelphia to face two murder charges and two attempted murder charges, including the shooting of Tazz that Peaches had put on him.

Chapter 22

Drake felt the sensation of someone bouncing on the bed. He opened his eyes and saw a little boy jumping up and down on the bed and holding some kind of action figure doll between his legs. He had to be about three years old, and he didn't look like anybody's child that Drake knew. Who little boy is this? Drake thought to himself. He sat up in the bed, and then took a good look around the room. He was no longer in the hospital, nor was he at home either. Where the hell am I? he wondered.

The bedroom was plush, complete with French doors leading to a balcony. He was laying on a king size bed with a canopy over it. On the cream wall over the fireplace was a large painting of a man and woman, holding a small child. On the opposite wall was a 60-inch flat screen TV that was showing cartoons, compliments of the kid.

Covering the floor in front of the fireplace was a large zebra fur rug with the head still attached to it, bringing out the cedar brook wood floor throughout the bedroom.

Off to the side of the room next to the spacious walk-in closet was a door leading to what appeared to be the bathroom, and some four feet from the bathroom door was a desk with a computer on top of it. There was a printer right beside it on a separate small table, and a fancy office chair in front of it.

The room was huge, bigger than some apartments. The ceiling was close to 12 ft. high, and the double doors leading to the rest of the house were mostly made of glass.

Drake didn't have a clue where he was until Cindy walked into the bedroom. She had on a pair of Kiss Me All Over pajama pants, a tank top, and a pair of Bugs Bunny slippers. Her hair was pulled into a ponytail, and in her hands were a couple of toys she had picked up off of the floor when she walked into the room. She looked like a rich but cute hood chick.

"Rodney, you know you can't be bouncing on my bed, now get down," she said, grabbing the remote control from off the nightstand. Little Rodney took off running at full speed out of the room, leaving his action figure doll behind.

Now knowing where he was, Drake still didn't understand how and why he was at her place. For the past few days he'd been sleeping deeply even though he had been fully out of his coma for a few weeks now.

"I got one word for you," she said, sitting next to him on the bed. "Insurance; when you don't have medical insurance, the hospital's job is to get you stabilized enough to send you home. You had to have a couple of surgeries to get the bullet out of your spine. I guess the doctors felt that they did enough work for free. When I came to see you the other day, the doctor said that he was going to discharge you, and that somebody had to sign you out because you were in stable condition. Your aunt Jackie was coming down with the flu, so I told her that I would take care of everything and for her to call me when she felt better."

"How long have I been here?" Drake asked.

"You've been here for almost a week. Five days to be exact. The doctor said you would be doing a lot of sleeping for a couple of days. I had my sister, Alisha, feed you when you woke up for short periods of time during the day. You ate a lot of baby food," she said, smiling at the thought of it.

Drake did remember a couple of times waking up and being fed. He swore that it was a nurse shoving food down his throat. She even had the same type of food cart the nurses used when they fed their patients.

"How do you feel?" Cindy asked in a soft tone. "The doctor said that your spine was bruised pretty badly, but that with therapy you'll be back to walking again."

Drake looked down at his feet and smiled when he moved his toes a little. He still didn't have much feeling in his legs, but at least he knew that he wasn't permanently paralyzed. The pain in his back was excruciating at times, but today he was able to sit up in the bed. "My back hurts like hell," he said, reaching for the pills on the nightstand that he hoped were for pain. "Do you always bring strange men home from the hospital?" he asked with a smile on his face.

"Only the ones who save my life." She smiled. "I thought the least I could do for you was to give you a safe place for you to rest; and for the record, the only man that ever slept in this bed was the one who just shot out of this room leaving his toys behind."

They both shared a smile. Drake wanted to chuckle, but it would hurt too much. They sat there for a moment and shared eye contact until he reached over and put his hand on Cindy's hand. "Thank you," he said in a sincere manner, then placed his hand back on his lap. "So, who's the kid?" he asked.

Cindy hesitated for a second, took in a deep breath and went with her gut instincts, telling herself that Drake would pose no threat to little Rodney. "He's my son. His name is Rodney, and before you ask, his dad died a few years ago. Most people don't even know that he exists. It's the streets, you know. I don't want anybody trying to hurt him because of what I do for a living. I try my best to keep my personal life separate from my street life."

The statement Cindy made hit Drake hard. It made him feel the burden of responsibility for the death of Kim and his son. He wanted to cry, but he held back his tears, realizing that there was nothing he could do to bring them back. By God's will he was still alive. This gave him all the motivation in the world to push himself to get back on his feet again in order to find Villain; that was until he realized he had already been caught.

It became apparent to Cindy that this was the first time Drake heard about Villain being in custody from the way he froze when the news anchor came on the television.

"...Vincent Thompson will be arraigned tomorrow morning for the shooting deaths of Kimberly Simmons, her newborn son, and the attempted murder of her fiancé whose name is being withheld. He is also being charged with the attempted murder of a young woman by the name of Danika Summers, whose throat he allegedly cut and left for dead in Fairmount Park a little over a month ago."

"We will bring you more on this story, and of further allegations regarding another attempted murder by Vincent Thompson as it unfolds."

Drake couldn't take his eyes off of the television screen. His hopes of killing Villain were shattered, and that in itself was enough for the tears to actually begin to fall down his face. It even gave him enough strength to slightly move one of his legs.

Cindy could sense the pain Drake was feeling in his heart, and she had to stop herself from crying too by getting up and walking out of the room. For some crazy reason she wanted to help him. She wanted to do something for him, but she couldn't. Feeling helpless was one of the worst emotions in the world, and that's a feeling both Cindy and Drake equally shared at that moment. If she could, she would have had one of her shooters blow Villain's head off, not just for Drake, but also for Kim and the baby. Family was one thing that meant everything to Cindy.

Christina rushed to answer the phone before the answering machine switched on. When she answered, an operator asked if she would accept a collect call from Vincent Thompson, aka Villain. At first she didn't want to accept the call, thinking about how cruel he was to kill a woman and her child. There weren't too many people who could accept something like that, but Christina's personal feelings didn't have anything to do with the relationship that he and Tazz had. Plus, if it weren't for Villain, Tazz would be six feet under. Her feelings were very much distorted about Villain, but through it all, she accepted the call.

"How are you, Vince?" she answered, walking from the kitchen into the living room.

"I could be better. I'm supposed to be going to court in a couple of days. I was wondering if you could be there. I mean, I can understand if you don't want to come. It just… I need to see a familiar face. I need you to be there so I can be reminded of why I put myself here."

Christina didn't know what to say. I'm not the reason you shot all those people, she thought to herself. "I don't understand," she said, not sure where he was going with all this.

"You know Tazz was my best friend. I would do anything for him, and I know how much he loved you. Seeing you would remind me of him, and with that my regrets would be suppressed. I can't do but so much talking over the phone, so if I see you in court I'd like to thank you in advance. And if I don't see you, I'll understand."

"Vincent, wait. I think there's somebody here you might want to talk to," Christina said, handing the phone over to Tazz.

Villain had no idea that Tazz was still alive. He was just about to ask Christina for an obituary for Tazz and the location of his burial. He'd been on the run since the shooting and really didn't have time to watch the news or check up on him, so when he heard Tazz's voice on the other end of the phone, he momentarily dropped the receiver.

"Hello, friend," Tazz whispered into the phone after trying to clear the phlegm from his throat.

"Boy, you don't know how happy I am to hear your voice. I swear, when I dropped you off at the hospital I thought you were already dead." A feeling of relief came over Villain, and even the possibility of getting out of jail raced through his mind, knowing that Tazz was still alive and on the streets.

This phone call was too overwhelming for him, considering some of the harsh conditions he was going through in the jail and in the courtroom. "They got me in protective custody right now, bro. The warden said my case is too high profile for me to be in population."

"What about court? When is your next court date?" Tazz asked, trying to keep his conversation limited. There was a lot he wanted to talk to Villain about, and unlike Christina and everybody else who disliked Villain, Tazz was okay with what he had done.

"The public defender said I go on Monday."

"Public defender?" Tazz asked, shocked at the fact he didn't have a paid lawyer. "Look, this is what I want you to do. Don't say another word to the public defender. I'll see you in court on Monday, ya hear me?"

"Yeah, I hear you."

"One more thing," Tazz said, before hanging up the phone. "Thank you."

The kind of relationship that Tazz and Villain shared was like no other. They were childhood best friends, vowing to always be there for one another, as they got older. They were tighter than most blood brothers, and no matter what, Tazz was not going to let Villain sit in jail to rot, at least not without doing anything and everything he could to get him out. He especially wasn't going to let him be represented by the public defender's office. Being represented by them in a capital murder case would definitely guarantee a guilty verdict within a couple of hours of deliberation. Tazz wasn't going to let Villain go out like that. Not on his watch.

Chapter 23

Hassan finished the Jumar prayer and immediately left the building with a lot on his mind. He jumped into his car, took his kufi off and grabbed the Glock .40 from under his seat, making sure that he had a bullet in the chamber before he pulled off.

He had a meeting with Cindy in about an hour to discuss whether or not he was going to participate in "Operation Takeover". His involvement in the streets was limited, but his name was well-known and feared throughout the city, which made him a prime candidate in Cindy's eyes to partner up with. Cindy offered him 50/50 on all profits as long as he pulled his own weight and shared the responsibility of maintaining order in the streets.

This was the area Hassan struggled in over the past month, trying to balance being a Muslim and also being a drug dealer, which would never be accepted in the eyes of his Creator. Like many young Muslims in the city of Philadelphia who are upon the Salaf, i.e., the rightly guided Muslims, Hassan lacked in being obedient to Allah, and found himself clinging to the worldly things that are forbidden in Islam. Such things are fast money, fast cars, and fast women—all which would be coming from pure cocaine being fast tracked through the turnpike by a fast-talking Hispanic kid.

Hassan pulled up to the Outback Steakhouse on Baltimore Pike and saw that Cindy was already there because her truck was in the parking lot. He never went to too many places without it, so the Glock .40 was placed on his hip as a soon as he got out of the car.

Cindy was sitting in a booth in the back of the restaurant when Hassan entered. The smell of the food throughout the place made him hungry, although eating wasn't his intention during this meeting.

"Cuz!" Cindy said, getting up to give him a hug. "I see you did the Muslim thing today," she said, noticing the strong sweet smell of the prayer oil he was wearing. "I didn't order yet. I was waiting until you came in just in case you were hungry."

Even though Hassan was hungry, he refused to order anything, wanting only to discuss business. Cindy, on the other hand, ordered a boneless chicken breast and a Strawberry Daiquiri to wash it down. Before she began talking, she took a good look around the room to make sure nobody was eavesdropping on their conversation. "Look, cuz, I got a good connect that can supply anything I ask for," she said, leaning over the table to avoid having to talk loudly. "I got workers on almost every corner in South Philly, plus I knocked off a lot of competition along the way, both high and low level—"

"So what do you need me for?" Hassan interrupted, wanting Cindy to get to the position she wanted him to play.

"Let me be honest wit' you. I really don't need you, and I mean that with all due respect. Seeing as you're like the only blood I have left from my family tree here in the city, I figure I'd put you on first before I look to anybody else. You watched me grow up, and I watched you put in a lot of work during those times. But I never saw you get a lot of money. No disrespect. I feel that if anybody should be rich, driving around in nice cars, living in a nice home, and never having to struggle again in life, it should be you."

A lot of the things that Cindy was saying were more than just true; they were fact. Hassan occupied most of his life on the streets with shootings, fist fighting, and robbing people who weren't worth robbing. He never had more than 30 grand in his possession at one time, and he never could keep more than 30 grand in his possession for more than 24 hours. What he did manage to do was instill fear into the hearts of the weak, and gain the respect of the men who understood him. If you mentioned his name to anyone in any part of South Philly, it was guaranteed that the person knew exactly who you were talking about.

"I'm not tryin' to make a career out of this," Hassan said, turning his head to watch the waitress bringing water and breadsticks to the table.

"Me, either. But for right now I'm tryin' to secure my financial future. There's millions of dollars floating around out there, and I sure could use it. And I know you could, too. Look, I'm not tryin' to get you to do something you don't want to do. All I'm trying to do is offer you a piece of the pie."

Hassan sat back in the booth, thinking about everything Cindy had on the table, and whether or not it was worth disobeying Allah (God). The fear of Allah was in his heart, but not as much as it should have been.

"I'ma ride wit' you until the end of the summer, then after that, I'm out," he said, finally making up his mind. "I hope you're right about everything you're saying."

"Don't worry. By the end of the summer you'll be on the top ten list of the richest people in the city," Cindy said, raising her glass of water for a toast. "Now I'm hungry as hell! Where the fuck is my food?" she joked.

After leaving the restaurant, Cindy headed over to Rick's house to deliver the drugs he asked to buy for somebody else. The person wanted 18 ounces of powder, and Rick already had the money. She wished Rick wasn't on house arrest so he could take up some of the slack with larger weight sales. It seemed like throughout the day everybody wanted to buy large amounts of cocaine, and that meant Cindy wasted most of her day attending to their needs.

She pulled up to Rick's house within twenty minutes of leaving the restaurant and saw that he was already standing in the doorway waiting for her. A few things stood out that caught Cindy's attention as she got closer to him. It was obvious he was sweating like he just got finished jogging eight miles in 100-degree weather. He didn't make eye contact the entire time and when he spoke, he stuttered, something he never did.

"You alright?" Cindy asked, pulling the cocaine out and putting it on the table after they entered the house.

"Yeah, yeah, yeah, I'm good. I just ate something bad that my stomach's not agreeing with. Did you bring the hard?"

"Hard? You didn't ask me for hard," she said, now wondering why he was asking crazy questions and talking so loudly.

"My bad, I thought I told you to bring two ounces of hard with you; don't worry about it. I'll get it from you later."

When he pulled out the money, the bills were crisp and new. They were stuck together as if they just came off the printing press, and smelled like they hadn't been circulated yet. It took ten minutes for Rick to count out five grand.

Dis nigga is acting funny, Cindy thought to herself, wrapping up the deal and tucking the money into her back pocket. Her instincts told her that Rick might be using. She didn't think that he was smoking crack, but in South Philly, a lot of young guys were snorting cocaine. If she found out that Rick was one of them, he would be kicked off of the team. She had a zero tolerance for using the same drugs you were selling. She frowned upon smoking weed too, but allowed it.

"You get some sleep," Cindy told him with an attitude, hoping that he got the memo that she knew something was wrong with him. "And take the trash out. It's starting to stink in here," she said, before leaving the house and jumping into her car.

Agents Pesco and Lavinski tailed Cindy all day watching her every move, including the numerous drug transactions she made almost each time she pulled over.

The case that they were building on her was growing faster than they expected, and the confidential informant was successful in buying a brick of powder in about a week's time. She didn't even notice the increase of the informant's purchases. She was moving so much product it prevented her from keeping track.

Most dealers who are high up on the totem pole in the drug trafficking business become lazy, and the large amounts of money being made sometimes make them arrogant and cocky. When this happens, they let their guard down and become more concerned about the perks of being somewhat rich, and they forget about the importance of being aware of the law enforcement agencies that want to take them down. When they do let their guard down, that's when federal agents like Pesco and Lavinski are at their best.

They watched her as she left Rick's house and went straight to 20th and Carpenter Street, where a familiar face jumped into her truck. If the feds wanted to, they could have easily pulled Cindy's truck over and found enough evidence to indict her federally. But doing so just wasn't the way the feds worked, especially if they had it out for you.

The deal between Cindy and Mike lasted the length of the agents going around the block one time, and when Mike got out of the car, he was carrying a black plastic carry bag, which he immediately took into one of the houses on the block.

Instead of following Cindy, they sat and waited for Mike to come back outside of the house. This tactic was also a successfully proven method of building a strong case against someone. When Mike came back outside with the same black bag and got into his car, Agent Pesco pulled up next to him, pinning him in so that Mike couldn't do too much running. Pesco jumped out of his car, drew his gun and held it by his side. The sight of a white man in a suit and carrying a gun made the other drug dealers on the corner observing what was going on break out running. Pesco calmly walked over to Mike's car and tapped on his window with his gun for Mike to roll his window down.

"Can I help you, officer?" Mike said, after rolling down his window and taking a good look around to see if anybody was standing outside watching what was going on.

"I'm willing to bet anything that if I search your car right now, I'd be taking you to jail today," Pesco said, also looking around to see who was still outside. "You don't wanna go to jail, do you?"

"Man, what do you want?" Mike sighed, becoming irritated by Pesco's tone of voice.

"I want you to follow me," Pesco said, then walked off and jumped back into his car.

Mike's heart was racing the entire time. He was hoping that Pesco didn't search his car. If he did, he would have found two twin Glock 9mms, 18 ounces of powder he just bought off of Cindy, and 4½ ounces of crack he was about to drop off to his cousin in North Philadelphia. He could tell by Pesco's suit and demeanor that he wasn't a local narcotics detective. He must be some type of federal agent, he thought to himself as he watched Pesco pull off.

Mike took in a deep breath. He didn't want to follow him, but he decided that it might be in his best interest to find out what these people wanted. But before he pulled off to follow Pesco, he grabbed the two guns from under his seat, placed them in the black bag with the drugs and tossed it out of the window. He then yelled for his only worker that didn't run to come get it and hold it until he got back. Mike had no intentions of following the feds with a car full of drugs and guns in tow.

Chapter 24

Monday morning came quickly. Cindy walked out of the guest bedroom where she had slept, and went down the hallway to her bedroom where Drake had been sleeping for the past couple of weeks. Surprisingly, Drake was sitting up on the edge of the bed with his feet on the floor, showing little Rodney how to hold his hands when boxing. It was something Cindy had never seen before. Rodney never liked men outside of his father, of whom he had only seen in pictures.

"Mommy, look! I'm learning how to fight!" little Rodney said proudly of his newfound sport.

"Alright, Mike Tyson, I think you should be getting ready for school," Cindy said, tapping him on the butt as he ran past her.

"You got a good kid. He's going to be tough just like you when he gets older," Drake said as he rubbed his thighs trying to get some feeling in them. "I got to go downtown today, so I was wondering if you could drop me off. You don't have to wait for me though. I'ma try to get a ride to my house a little later."

"So you're going home for good?" she asked as if she really didn't want him to leave just yet. She was starting to get used to Drake lying up in her bed, even though his movements were limited. It was nice to have someone to talk to at night when she got home from a long day.

Also, there was something about Drake that made her feel comfortable. She didn't think too much about men and the possibility of getting involved with another one again, but having a very handsome and somewhat physically capable man lying in her bed—and one with whom she was able to confide in with some of her most intimate thoughts—made the idea tempting. "I got something I need to take care of at my house and I can't put it off any longer," Drake said, thinking about the two hundred bricks of cocaine and the other millions in cash that he took from Tazz. Drake knew that Cindy was dealing in drugs, but he didn't know to what extent. She didn't talk about it much during their late night conversations. Clearly, she was doing something right, considering the nice house she was living in, the car she was driving and all the expensive clothes in her closet. For some reason, he trusted her in the same manner that she trusted him, and for that reason Drake considered long and hard telling Cindy about the two hundred bricks.

The courtroom was packed with people. Reporters, supporters, and a lot of Kim's family were there awaiting Villain's arrival for his arraignment.

Tazz rolled into the courtroom with Christina pushing his wheelchair. He was there for a couple of reasons. One was to clear up any accusations about Villain being the one who shot him in Peaches' apartment; and the other reason was so that he could support Villain and possibly be ready to pay any kind of bail the judge was willing to hand out, if he decided to do so.

This case was very complicated, and counting everything that Villain was charged with, it would make anybody dizzy just hearing them. Most of the charges would be dismissed today due to one technicality or another, as is in almost every case.

Who Tazz didn't expect to see was Drake wheeling himself into the courtroom with Cindy by his side. They stared at one another from opposite sides of the courtroom, sharing the same amount of hate and desire to kill one another on sight. Neither one of them said a word. It wasn't until the judge finally came into the courtroom that they took their eyes off each other and focused in on what the judge was saying.

Villain wasn't the first case to be heard, so the DA took the time out to speak with both Tazz and Drake, since they both would be the star witnesses. Their interviews lasted just minutes, after which the DA quickly sat back down in his chair.

Two cases later, Villain's name was called and everybody in the courtroom froze.

"The Commonwealth vs. Vincent Thompson!" the

judge announced in a stern voice and lifted his head up from the docket sheet in front of him.

Villain stepped out of the holding cell behind the courtroom wearing a blue, two-piece jail uniform that looked like nurse's scrubs, and a pair of blue bus shoes. His hair was unkempt, and it looked like he lost a ton of weight in the past couple of weeks. All in all, he looked bad. He promptly took a seat at the table where all defendants sat with their lawyers during the proceedings.

The sight of Villain sparked a fury inside of Drake that was indescribable, and it showed the way that he stared at him. Now there were two people in the courtroom that Drake wanted to kill. Tazz sat with a smirk on his face, imagining how Drake must be feeling.

The judge went down the long list of charges brought against Villain by the state; to which Villain plead not guilty to each and every one of them. His lawyer was a female named Cathy Martin; a well-known lawyer in the city who had numerous not guilty verdicts under her belt for robbery, attempted murder, and murder itself. Although she was a petite blond with large voluptuous breasts and a pretty smile, she was well aware of the law and could attack in the courtroom with precision like a female lion hunting for her prey. If the state had any plans on winning their case, they had better pack their lunch and dinner going up against her.

"On the charges of attempted murder on the life of Terrance Good, does the state have any witnesses?" the judge asked the DA.

"Yes, Your Honor; the state calls the victim, Terrance Good," the DA responded.

Christine pushed Tazz to the front of the courtroom where he placed his hand on the Bible and swore to tell the truth.

Drake looked on in disgust and fear that Tazz would point him out as being the one who shot him. Tazz stared back at Drake, as if letting him know he was about to spill it all.

The DA asked him a few questions about who he was for identification purposes for the court, and then she got right down to business.

"Mr. Good, were you in the apartment of a woman known to you as Peaches?"

"Yes, I was."

"And can you explain what happened on that day?"

"Yes. I was shot and robbed for my money."

"Is the person who shot you in this courtroom today?"

The courtroom was quiet, and everybody was expecting for him to say that it was Villain who shot him. He looked to the back of the courtroom to make eye contact with Drake, and then winked his left eye at him.

Drake braced himself to be arrested immediately, but what happened next shocked the entire courtroom. "No. The person who shot me is not in the courtroom today," Tazz said, turning his attention back to the DA.

The courtroom became loud with people whispering to one another and gasping in disbelief. The DA was shocked, thinking that she and Tazz had an understanding that Villain was the shooter. The judge had to call for order in the courtroom several times before the room became silent again.

To be sure, the DA asked Tazz the question again, but this time warning him not to try and take justice into his own hands. Again, Tazz's answer was the same.

"So just to be clear, my client, Vincent Thompson was not the man who shot you?" Villain's lawyer asked on cross-examination.

"Yes, that's correct," Tazz said, while shooting a glance in Drake's direction to let him know that he wasn't a rat.

That one look after not pointing him out as the shooter let Drake know that Tazz wanted to settle his beef on the streets and not in the courtroom. This was something that was understood amongst street dwellers.

"Do you have any more witnesses?" the judge asked the DA, letting her know that she needed to move forward with her case.

"Yes, Your Honor. We have Danika Summers."

Peaches entered the courtroom from outside in the hallway, escorted by a detective. When she saw Drake sitting in the wheelchair, her heart froze and tears began to flow from her eyes. She didn't know that he was going to be there, and seeing him brought up many mixed emotions. She was happy to see him, but felt like she had betrayed him by telling Villain where he was, which ultimately ended up in the deaths of Kim and his baby. She sat on the witness stand wiping the tears from her eyes. Now that she had not only seen Drake, but also Tazz, she didn't know what to say.

"Ms. Summers, do you see the man who cut your throat in the courtroom today?" the DA asked, hoping that she didn't recant her statement, too. She didn't. As soon as Peaches laid eyes on Villain for the first time, she pointed his ass out before the DA could finish asking the question.

Again, the people in the courtroom got loud, and the judge had to call for order. The lies were coming a mile a minute as Peaches told the story of how two people broke into her apartment while she and Tazz were asleep in bed. One of the guys was Villain, and she didn't know the other guy. She said that they robbed Tazz for his money, shot him, and then kidnapped her for ransom. She said that she didn't see exactly who shot Tazz because she was tied up and put into the trunk of Villain's car. She knew for sure that Villain was the one who cut her throat in the park and left her for dead. She said he did it because her ex-boyfriend, Drake, wouldn't pay the ransom for her when she called him because he was in the hospital with his current girlfriend about to have a baby. She said Villain told her he was going to kill her and then go to the hospital and kill Drake for not paying the ransom.

Not one time did Peaches stutter while making up this story, and according to her testimony she didn't contradict Tazz's testimony either. She was sharp, and she never took her eyes off of Villain the entire time.

Ms. Martin, Villain's lawyer wasted no time in digging into Peaches' story and aggressively attacking her credibility. "Ms. Summers, something doesn't sit well with me. I know this isn't a trial, but I'm just curious. You're saying that my client, Vincent Thompson, the best friend of Terrence Good—who is in court today—robbed him, shot him, and cut your throat because your ex-boyfriend wouldn't pay your ransom?"

Ms. Martin was a trial expert, and she knew how to find holes in statements from would-be witnesses that would end up biting them in the ass later on. It was a strategy she was good at, and for the most part she did it better than 90% of the lawyers in the city. She questioned Peaches to the point where Peaches didn't want to answer her anymore because she wanted details about each and every thing.

Understanding that this was just a hearing, Villain's lawyer let up, saving the juicier details in the event this case went to trial. Of course, she would be filing many, many motions to dismiss a lot of the charges due to the lack of evidence.

Martin was probably the best thing that Villain had on his side, but the day was still young, and the DA's office still had a huge bomb to drop after the fifteen-minute recess the judge ordered for bathroom breaks.

"All rise!" the clerk announced as the judge walked back into the courtroom.

Everyone was still in the same places they were before the break, not even getting up to use the bathroom for fear that they might miss something or lose their seats. Peaches, on the other hand, was escorted out of the courtroom by the same detective that brought her there, seeing as she was now in the Witness Protection Program.

"The state can call their next witness," the judge said, leaning back in his chair, waiting to see who would testify next.

They called someone from the hospital. It was a security guard who testified regarding the surveillance photos that only caught a fuzzy image of Villain's face in one photo, and a clearer shot of his backside as he walked out of the emergency exit. He also testified to catching a glimpse of Villain with his own eyes, but he wasn't too sure if he could identify him with certainty.

The witnesses continued to pour in, all of which were on the same floor when the shooting occurred. The only problem was that nobody could positively identify Villain as being the shooter, mainly because their heads were on the floor at the time, or they had ducked behind something for cover. This kind of evidence was circumstantial at best, and wasn't enough to hold a man for trial, or so Villain and Tazz hoped.

What came now was the only man who would be able to pinpoint and positively identify Villain as the one who killed his fiancée and his newborn child. This was the one man who could surely put Villain away for the rest of his life, or possibly get him the death penalty. He could get payback for all the pain Villain put him through, and also bring closure to Kim's family for the devastating losses. It was his chance to finally look into the eyes of the man who took everything from him.

"The state calls Derrick Henson," the DA announced, smiling at the fact that Drake was willing to testify.

You could hear the people in the room whispering to one another as Drake rolled himself to the front of the courtroom.

Being able to finally lay his eyes on Villain was one of the most intense moments of Drake's life. It wasn't until Villain picked his head up and looked him directly in his eyes that Drake almost lost it. He bit down on his bottom lip and gave Villain a look that spelled out the words, "I'm going to kill you." The fury inside of Drake boiled to the point he didn't even hear the DA asking him any questions.

"Mr. Henson is the man who shot you and murdered your fiancée and newborn son in this courtroom today?" the DA asked in an aggressive manner in hopes it would snap him out of his trance.

The courtroom was so quiet while everybody was tuned in to hear what Drake was about to say. Even the judge sat patiently and awaited his answer.

So much was running through Drake's mind. Villain had to pay for what he'd done to his family, and nothing would get in his way. He thought about all the people who were going to hate him for what he was about to do, but no one could ever understand the way he felt, so what other people thought really meant nothing to him. "No!" Drake said, finally breaking the stare between him and Villain and turning to look at the DA.

The courtroom became loud all over again to the point where the judge couldn't get order right away. The DA just threw her hands in the air in a gesture that meant she was giving up.

Kim's mother screamed at Drake, "What are you doin'? What are you doin'? He killed your baby! He killed my baby!"

Villain turned to his lawyer in shock, and then looked back at Tazz who was sitting in his wheelchair with a smile on his face, also shocked by what Drake had just said. Everybody in the courtroom was shocked, even the judge.

Drake glanced back and forth from Villain to Tazz, declaring a war on both men without having to say a word. The pleasure of him knowing that court would be held on the streets was satisfaction in itself. There wasn't a place in this world that Villain could hide, and Drake was going to do anything and everything in his power to see that he would die in the worst way. Drake had 200 bricks of cocaine and millions in cash to see that it happened.

The fire inside of Drake gave him enough energy and power to rise slowly from out of the wheelchair he was sitting in. This was the first time he was able to stand on his own since the incident. At first he couldn't feel much in his legs, but the pressure he felt in his back from the gunshot wound sent a sharp pain all the way down to his feet.

Villain thought that Drake would be stupid and charge at him out of anger, but he was wrong. Drake gave him a crooked smile then took his first baby step in the opposite direction. The pain was even worse trying to walk, but it didn't matter to him because there was no physical pain known to man that could equal to the mental anguish he was feeling. He wanted to let Villain and Tazz know that three bullets in his back and one in his chest only slowed him down instead of shutting him down.

Cindy rushed to the front of the courtroom when she saw that Drake was struggling with walking. She threw his arm over her shoulder, placed her arm around his waist, and helped him walk slowly out of the courtroom, leaving the wheelchair behind. As everyone in court watched him leave, Drake was preparing for the ultimate war. Mentally, he was ready and with Cindy's help and his own sheer determination to extract revenge, soon Drake would be physically ready, too.

Drake Part 2 Now Available!

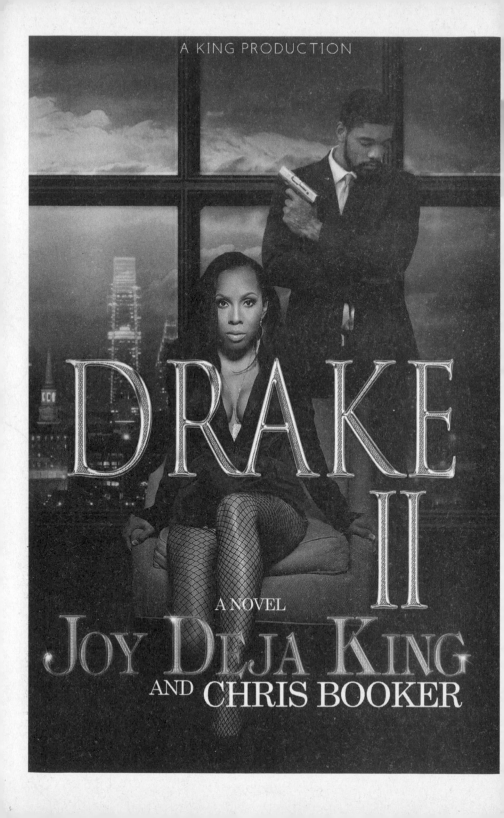

A KING PRODUCTION

DRAKE II

A NOVEL

JOY DEJA KING
AND CHRIS BOOKER

A KING PRODUCTION

Power

NO ONE MAN SHOULD HAVE ALL THAT POWER...BUT THERE WERE TWO

JOY DEJA KING

Chapter 1
UNDERGROUND KING

Alex stepped into his attorney's office to discuss what was always his number one priority...business. When he sat down their eyes locked and there was complete silence for the first few seconds. This was Alex's way of setting the tone of the meeting. His silence spoke volumes. This might've been his attorney's office but he was the head nigga in charge and nothing got started until he decided it was time to speak. Alex felt this approach was necessary. You see, after all these years of them doing business, attorney George Lofton still wasn't used to dealing with a man like Alex; a dirt-poor kid who could've easily died in the projects he was born in, but instead had made millions. It wasn't done the ski mask way but it was still illegal.

They'd first met when Alex was a sixteen-year-old kid growing up in TechWood Homes, a housing project in Atlanta. Alex and his best friend, Deion, had been arrested because the principal found 32 crack vials in Alex's book bag. Another kid had tipped the principal off and the principal subsequently called the police. Alex and Deion were arrested and suspended from school. His mother called George, who had the charges against them dismissed, and they were allowed to go back to school. But that wasn't the last time he would use George. He was arrested at twenty-two for attempted murder, and for trafficking cocaine a year later. Alex was acquitted on both charges. George Lofton later became known as the best trial attorney in Atlanta, but Alex had also become the best at what he did. And since it was Alex's money that kept Mr. Lofton in designer suits, million dollar homes and foreign cars, he believed he called the shots, and dared his attorney to tell him otherwise.

Alex noticed that what seemed like a long period of silence made Mr. Lofton feel uncomfortable, which he liked. Out of habit, in order to camouflage the discomfort, his attorney always kept bottled water within arm's reach. He would cough, take a swig, and lean back in his chair, raising his eyebrows a little, trying to give a look of certainty, though he wasn't completely confident at all in Alex's presence. The reason was because Alex did what many had thought would be impossible, especially men like George Lofton. He had gone from a knucklehead, low-level drug dealer to an underground king and an unstoppable respected criminal boss.

Before finally speaking, Alex gave an intense stare into George Lofton's piercing eyes. They were not only the bluest he had ever seen, but also some of the most calculating. The latter is what Alex found so compelling. A calculating attorney working on his behalf could almost guarantee a get out of jail free card for the duration of his criminal career.

"Have you thought over what we briefly discussed the other day?" Alex asked his attorney, finally breaking the silence.

"Yes I have, but I want to make sure I understand you correctly. You want to give me six hundred thousand to represent you or your friend Deion if you are ever arrested and have to stand trial again in the future?"

Alex assumed he had already made himself clear based on their previous conversations and was annoyed by what he now considered a repetitive question. "George, you know I don't like repeating myself. That's exactly what I'm saying. Are we clear?"

"So this is an unofficial retainer."

"Yes, you can call it that."

George stood and closed the blinds then walked over to the door that led to the reception area. He turned the deadbolt so they wouldn't be disturbed. George sat back behind the desk. "You know that if you and your friend Deion are ever on the same case that I can't represent the both of you."

"I know that."

"So what do you propose I do if that was ever to happen?"

"You would get him the next best attorney in Atlanta," Alex said without hesitation. Deion was Alex's best friend—had been since the first grade. They were now business partners, but the core of their bond was built on that friendship, and because of that Alex would always look out for Deion's best interest.

"That's all I need to know."

Alex clasped his hands and stared at the ceiling for a moment, thinking that maybe it was a bad idea bringing the money to George. Maybe he should have just put it somewhere safe only known to him and his mom. He quickly dismissed his concerns.

"Okay. Where's the money?" Alex presented George with two leather briefcases. He opened the first one and was glad to see that it was all hundred-dollar bills. When he closed the briefcase he asked, "There is no need to count this is there?"

"You can count it if you want, but it's all there."

George took another swig of water. The cash made him nervous. He planned to take it directly to one of his bank safe deposit boxes. The two men stood. Alex was a foot taller than George; he had flawless mahogany skin, a deep brown with a bit of a red tint, broad shoulders, very large hands, and a goatee. He was a man's man. With such a powerful physical appearance, Alex kept his style very low-key. His only display of wealth was a pricey diamond watch that his best friend and partner Deion had bought him for his birthday.

"I'll take good care of this, and you," his attorney said, extending his hand to Alex.

"With this type of money, I know you will," Alex stated without flinching. Alex gave one last lingering stare into his attorney's piercing eyes. "We do have a clear understanding...correct?"

"Of course. I've never let you down and I never will. That, I promise you." The men shook hands and

Alex made his exit with the same coolness as his entrance.

With Alex embarking on a new, potentially dangerous business venture, he wanted to make sure that he had all his bases covered. The higher up he seemed to go on the totem pole, the costlier his problems became. But Alex welcomed new challenges because he had no intention of ever being a nickel and dime nigga again.

A KING PRODUCTION

Power 2

NO ONE MAN SHOULD HAVE ALL THAT POWER...BUT THERE WERE TWO

JOY DEJA KING

A KING PRODUCTION

Baller
Bitches
VOLUME 3
PARTS 7-10

A NOVEL

JOY DEJA KIN

Order Form
A King Production
P.O. Box 912
Collierville, TN 38027
www.joydejaking.com
www.twitter.com/joydejaking

Name: _____

Address: _____

City/State: • _____

Zip: _____

QUANTITY	TITLES	PRICE	TOTAL
_____	Bitch	$15.00	_____
_____	Bitch Reloaded	$15.00	_____
_____	The Bitch Is Back	$15.00	_____
_____	Queen Bitch	$15.00	_____
_____	Last Bitch Standing	$15.00	_____
_____	Superstar	$15.00	_____
_____	Ride Wit' Me	$12.00	_____
_____	Stackin' Paper	$15.00	_____
_____	Trife Life To Lavish	$15.00	_____
_____	Trife Life To Lavish II	$15.00	_____
_____	Stackin' Paper II	$15.00	_____
_____	Rich or Famous	$15.00	_____
_____	Rich or Famous Part 2	$15.00	_____
_____	Bitch A New Beginning	$15.00	_____
_____	Mafia Princess Part 1	$15.00	_____
_____	Mafia Princess Part 2	$15.00	_____
_____	Mafia Princess Part 3	$15.00	_____
_____	Mafia Princess Part 4	$15.00	_____
_____	Mafia Princess Part 5	$15.00	_____
_____	Boss Bitch	$15.00	_____
_____	Baller Bitches Vol. 1	$15.00	_____
_____	Baller Bitches Vol. 2	$15.00	_____
_____	Bad Bitch	$15.00	_____
_____	Still The Baddest Bitch	$15.00	_____
_____	Power	$15.00	_____
_____	Power Part 2	$15.00	_____
_____	Drake	$15.00	_____
_____	Drake Part 2	$15.00	_____
_____	Princess Fever "Birthday Bash"	$9.99	_____

Shipping/Handling (Via Priority Mail) $6.50 1-2 Books, $8.95 3-4 Books add $1.95 for ea. Additional book.

Total: $_____ **FORMS OF ACCEPTED PAYMENTS:** Certified or government issued checks and money Orders, all mail in orders take 5-7 Business days to be delivered

Order Form
A King Production
P.O. Box 912
Collierville, TN 38027
www.joydejaking.com
www.twitter.com/joydejaking

Name: _____

Address: _____

City/State: _____

Zip: _____

QUANTITY	TITLES	PRICE	TOTAL
_____	Bitch	$15.00	_____
_____	Bitch Reloaded	$15.00	_____
_____	The Bitch Is Back	$15.00	_____
_____	Queen Bitch	$15.00	_____
_____	Last Bitch Standing	$15.00	_____
_____	Superstar	$15.00	_____
_____	Ride Wit' Me	$12.00	_____
_____	Stackin' Paper	$15.00	_____
_____	Trife Life To Lavish	$15.00	_____
_____	Trife Life To Lavish II	$15.00	_____
_____	Stackin' Paper II	$15.00	_____
_____	Rich or Famous	$15.00	_____
_____	Rich or Famous Part 2	$15.00	_____
_____	Bitch A New Beginning	$15.00	_____
_____	Mafia Princess Part 1	$15.00	_____
_____	Mafia Princess Part 2	$15.00	_____
_____	Mafia Princess Part 3	$15.00	_____
_____	Mafia Princess Part 4	$15.00	_____
_____	Mafia Princess Part 5	$15.00	_____
_____	Boss Bitch	$15.00	_____
_____	Baller Bitches Vol. 1	$15.00	_____
_____	Baller Bitches Vol. 2	$15.00	_____
_____	Bad Bitch	$15.00	_____
_____	Still The Baddest Bitch	$15.00	_____
_____	Power	$15.00	_____
_____	Power Part 2	$15.00	_____
_____	Drake	$15.00	_____
_____	Drake Part 2	$15.00	_____
_____	Princess Fever "Birthday Bash"	$9.99	_____

Shipping/Handling (Via Priority Mail) $6.50 1-2 Books, $8.95 3-4 Books add $1.95 for ea. Additional book.

Total: $_____ **FORMS OF ACCEPTED PAYMENTS:** Certified or government issued checks and money Orders, all mail in orders take 5-7 Business days to be delivered

A KING PRODUCTION

Baller
Bitches
VOLUME 3
PARTS 7-10

A NOVEL

JOY DEJA KING